SUPREMACY

a novel by
K. M. Lovejoy

Supremacy

© 2017 by K. M. Lovejoy

ISBN: 978-1-941066-17-1

Library of Congress Control Number: 2017950997

Cover design by Mark Lapin

Photos on front and rear covers are of Mistress Amazon
(www.submittoamazon.com)

Book design by Jo-Anne Rosen

Wordrunner Press
Petaluma, California

To my partner for
his or her sense of humor

Contents

1

Leavings

I may have been naïve, but I knew better than to google "How to hire an assassin."

I had resurgent brain cancer – diffuse astrocytoma, a galaxy of tumors on the astrocytes, the star-shaped cells that make up the supportive tissue of the brain. I had nothing to lose.

Three years ago, I learned the astrocytoma had reached stage 3. It was inoperable because the tumors were in too deep – removing them would have made me a vegetable. I went for a heavy dose of chemo and radiation to prevent the cancer from spreading. Thank goodness for medical marijuana or I would not have survived the chemo. I shaved my head. I liked the androgynous look, even though my skull was not smooth like Mr. Clean, but bumpy like a golf ball.

After a reprieve, the biopsy came back positive a few weeks ago. My oncologist, a blond woman in her late thirties, recommended more chemo and radiation. I told her I would rather die.

"There's another possibility. It's a long shot. Injecting embryonic stem cells into the brain. But the cells must come from embryos created from your own sperm.

Unfortunately, Congress has outlawed creating embryos for research or therapy. The right's right to life idea. The appeals court threw out this restriction but: they ruled that no new embryos could be created until the Supreme Court rules on the appeal. You know the composition of the Court. It doesn't look good. Without this therapy, you have a year or two of intensifying headaches before your astrocytes are overwhelmed and your brain becomes mush. At which point you will die."

I liked her bluntness, but her words were spinning in my disease-addled brain. "A different Supreme Court might rule differently?"

"Of course."

I wanted a meaningful death. I wanted to make a difference. Someone had to do it. Someone had to arrange the assassination of one of the right-wing Supreme Court Justices. It might as well be me. And so dawned my mission for the rest of my life.

Why don't the "terrorists" and/or revolutionaries use old people for their suicide assaults? Why teenagers with their whole lives ahead of them?

I had ruled out doing the deed myself. I thought about it hard. I even dusted off my grandfather's World War I vintage .45 automatic and joined a local gun club for target practice. But I was a lousy shot no matter how much practice I got, and a bit of a klutz besides. Likely to fuck up so delicate an operation. Even more so with my star-studded brain imploding.

As soon as I made the decision, an urgency kicked in. I didn't have much time. Plus, in addition to the case prohibiting the creation of new embryos, three other critical cases were coming up on the court's calendar in the next eight months.

And my 30-year marriage was crumbling because of my porn addiction. I had met Mariana – like the trench – 30 years ago in Cuernavaca. I was studying Spanish; she was my teacher. I loved to brush her long black hair that swept all the way down her back. A touch of *indigena* blood darkened her skin, smooth as flan, a smoothness she claimed came from the collard greens a Black friend had told her to eat. Now a little over fifty, her body was graduating from slender to zaftig, a development she hated and whined about, but it gave her a softness that increased my lust for her even as she denied my access.

We had raised two daughters, Lupe and Marisol, now in their late 20s. Lupe a pediatrician, Marisol a fifth-grade teacher and collage artist. Great kids, smart and solid.

The sex between Mariana and me was ecstatic at first. Like most Mexicans, she was raised Catholic – thus both ardent in her sexuality, and vanilla. The ardency was enough for me, but after the girls were born, she lost interest. I became addicted to porn, mostly what they call the Femdom stuff – women dominating men. The reverse – men dominating women which reinforces the oppressive societal pattern, turned me off.

About ten years ago, before "alternative sexuality" had become mainstream, I was at my computer in the corner of the attic I had carved out as my study

– my garret, I liked to think of it – pretending to write my novel. That novel, what little I'd written, was an attempt to imagine what a revolution might look like in the U. S. *2020 Hindsight* was the working title. I had my pants down stroking myself when Mariana's head suddenly emerged up the pull-down trap door stairs. I pulled up my pants and switched screens on the computer, but the sound from the video continued, the crack of a whip, a man screaming. She looked at me with that parental frown reserved for times when I did something egregiously wrong. She grabbed the mouse and opened the screen to a woman all in leather whipping a man in manacles and fuchsia panties. "Really, Peter? That's disgusting. You're sick. And decadent! You're supposed to be this leftist and all, and this is how you treat me?"

Her words did sting. I started attending Sex Addicts Anonymous meetings. But she caught me arranging a meeting with a woman from OK Cupid who fashioned herself as a Domme looking for a sissy and she just lost it. I didn't follow up on the meeting, but Mariana moved to the guest bedroom, and a chill settled into our house.

She got a rescue dog – a huge thing, part St. Bernard, part Great Dane, and part miniature poodle. She named him Peter – a not so subtle hint that he was replacing me, though she kindly called him Pedro to avoid confusing us.

I thought my marriage was over. For all intents and purposes, so was my life.

It was morning when I decided to tell her. We lived in Oakland in a craftsman bungalow which, as an overly perfectionist carpenter, had taken me too many years to remodel. I stared at the twin lumps in her twin bed in the guest bedroom. The dog slept beside her, and weighed as much as she did, or used to. "Pedro!" I commanded. He didn't stir.

Finally, Mariana got what was happening. "Get down, Pedro." She nudged him and he complied.

Fully dressed in my usual 501s and black pocket T, I crawled into bed with her. She was always cold. She was buried under three blankets and a comforter despite our mild October climate.

"I'm going to do it, Mariana."

"Do what?" she asked with thirty years of marital indifference.

"Assassinate Sylvester Johnson."

"The Supreme Court Justice?"

"Yeah."

"The only Black one."

"It's not like the Black community will mourn him. He has about seven Black supporters. The rest of them will ask, 'Was he really Black?'"

"Still. Didn't you say that Black people have just as much right to be assholes as anyone else?"

"Yeah, but think how things could change if there was just a small shift on the Supreme Court. One case could give me access to the embryonic stem cells that could save my life, and Johnson is the strongest voice on the court opposed to that access."

"A small shift. Are you sure it's not just those little starbursts in your brain that are making you do this?"

There was a long silence.

"I get it – you want to leave me to go commit murder. You know they'll kill you, right? So you want to die to get the stem cells that could save your life? You do see the contradiction here, Peter?"

"I know, but I'm dying anyway. I might as well do something worthwhile with what's left of my life."

She erupted in tears. She hugged me. She kissed me. We entangled our tongues. She was all over me. She took charge. She ripped off my clothes. She tore off her flowered flannel night gown and her granny undies. She pushed me onto my back, straddled me, took my cock in her mouth – something she had tried just once before – and shmushed her pussy into my mouth. Had I died? Was I dreaming?

She sat on my cock and humped me moaning like an adolescent girl on a horse. We shuddered together in an orgasm that went on forever – which hadn't happened since our wedding night. It was all so unexpected and delightful that I really didn't want to leave anymore.

As we cuddled in the afterglow, she said, "Good luck, Peter," the indifference flooding back into her voice.

I had already bought my ticket to DC, back when we were estranged. So, ripping the newfound Velcro connection between us, I went.

2

Perfect

There was something liberating about staring death in the face. It focused my attention on what was important, and what wasn't. What was important was *meaning*. Above all, I wanted a meaningful death.

Before I was diagnosed, I'd been having headaches which were, literally, to die for. They were killers. I tried everything – Fiorinal, Codeine, Tramadol, OxyContin, and of course marijuana. Once, drifting off into narcotic haze, I had this flash of insight: *Life is death's dream*. What does that even mean? Life is death's dream. Whatever it meant, the concept did not reinforce the boundaries between life, death, and dreaming.

Regret from leaving Mariana felt like a bowling ball sewed into the small of my back. I kissed her good-bye at the BART station where she tearfully, but not too tearfully, dropped me off. This could be the last time I would ever see her. I could almost hear her sigh of relief as she drove away in the beat-up Honda, the ever-present Pedro jumping from the back seat to the front seat next to her. Into my seat.

At the airport, a patina of newness covered everything and everyone, like when the sun comes out on the city streets after days of rain. Liberating too was the air I was breathing, a true terrorist breezing through airport security as they gave me the usual OWG – old white guy – pass, no need to remove my shoes or belt. A giddiness came over me as I imagined wearing my mission behind my smile. If they only knew that this nondescript middle-aged man was about to change history. As I raised my arms Christ-like in the full body scanner, that line from the Dylan came to mind: "If my thought-dreams could be seen, they'd probably put my head in a guillotine." How long before they had that thought-dream reading machine?

That "what a great idea" reaction to my assassination idea might be different in the section of the country we coastal snobs call "flyover," representatives of which began swarming at the various gates, headed to Boise, Nashville, Cleveland.

I wondered how many of them shared my understanding that the Supreme Court had perpetrated a coup d'état halting the recounts. They flagrantly anointed George W. Bush despite him having lost the popular vote and. probably, the electoral college vote as well, had the Florida recount been allowed to go forward.

I stopped at the Starbucks and ordered a venti mocha, extra shot, no whip. I sucked up the chocolate covered caffeine as I waited.

I boarded the Southwest flight, always the cheapest, and squeezed into a narrow seat by the window.

A guy with pasty cheeks and a Midwestern comb-over squeezed in next to me. His blue Nike jogging suit smelled as if after his morning run instead of showering, he had drenched himself with Brut. I smiled tentatively, not wishing to engage him. I feigned sleep and imagined explaining to him how the court followed *Bush v. Gore* with many decisions that inched the country toward an undemocratic plutocracy. Shelby County v. Holder eviscerated the Voting Rights Act. Citizen's United classified corporations as people, unleashing an unlimited torrent of corporate money into the electoral process. Decisions like *McKlesky v. Kemp* that eliminated the right to claim racial discrimination in criminal prosecutions, which led to the mass incarceration of Black and Latino people. Every single one of these decisions passed by a 5-4 majority of the justices.

As the engines began their whine, I quietly killed myself, as I always do when I fly. If man was meant to fly... Even if my mission were to end with this plane crashing, I would still have had a good life. We're obviously here to propagate the species – I'd done my part. That wildcat carpenter's strike I led back in the seventies won a small wage increase. There were five pre-published novels I'd written – maybe Mariana will unearth them when I die and publish them. Thirty years of marriage – not to be sneezed at. Monogamous marriage for life was invented when people lived to be thirty, yet I had held on. A pang knifed through me, missing her already. Missing her indifference, as if it accentuated my difference – the difference I made in the world, such as it was.

I tried to focus on the notion that life is death's dream, meaning, I supposed, that when we crashed, I would wake up.

I closed my eyes and held my breath against the vision of a fiery explosion as the acceleration of the plane pressed my body into the seat-back. Planes usually crash right after takeoff, or right before landing. As much as I hated capitalism, I had to acknowledge that the jets it built crashed far more rarely than they used to, far more seldom than the shaky economic condition of the airlines should have predicted.

As the plane began to cruise, the disembodied voice told us we could use our electronic devices. One of my favorite things to do was to hyper-caffeinate on a plane and write on my laptop. Something about lack of distraction, no place to go to distract myself. *"Distracted, that's a funny word. Does anyone ever get 'tracted'? I'm gonna call the suicide hotline and ask them."* Homer Simpson.

My neighbor, about one pound below the requirement to buy two seats, was hogging my right armrest. Luckily, on the other side of him was a tiny Chinese woman. I had to twist about awkwardly to extract my trusty MacBook from my backpack. The space was too narrow to use the tray table, so I angled it on my lap. I knew what I wanted to write. If I was going to carry out my mission, I needed a cover story in order to get the information I would need.

I wrote: "I may have been naïve, but I knew better than to google 'How to hire an assassin.'"

"Whatcha writing?" my neighbor asked.

"I've writing a novel about an older guy with nothing to lose who decides to murder a Supreme Court justice."

His eyes lit up. "Really? Which one?"

"It's fiction. The Black one."

"Sylvester Johnson?"

"It's fiction. I'll change his name."

"Why him?"

"Makes for a meatier story, more nuanced."

"Sounds like a good story. Something needs to happen."

I was relieved that he was one of "us." So much for stereotypes. "There's a quartet of cases coming before the court in the next few months that could change everything."

"In real life or in your novel?"

I hesitated. "Both."

"I know about the Florida case."

"*Williams v. Florida*. The legislature took away the right to vote not just from convicted felons, but from people with two or more misdemeanor convictions."

"Terrible. I read that book about mass incarceration. Terrible."

"The Michelle Alexander one?"

"Yeah, that one about the new Jim Crow."

"You know what's going on then."

"More or less. I don't know about the other cases.

Is there one about *Roe v. Wade?*"

"Yes, they could finally overturn it completely, eliminate a woman's right to choose," I said. "There's a couple of other cases too, all to be decided by the end of June. One could eliminate the power of the federal government to regulate carbon emissions – eviscerate the EPA just as people are really noticing the effect of global climate change. The embryonic stem cell case directly affects me. If things keep going like it looks like they're going, by July, we'll be in deep shit."

"What do you mean by deep shit?"

"Even more like a police state."

"A police state? Whatcha talking about?"

I suddenly wanted to write. The temperature of this interaction was dropping. "You know a dictatorship? Something like fascism? Mussolini?"

"In America? What are you, some kind of Communist?"

I guess I had misjudged the guy. "Excuse me, I need to work."

"Well, I'm not going to let you write that vicious propaganda. I'm gonna talk your ear off. It's my patriotic duty."

"Really?"

He stared at me. Cold and hard. Then he melted into a pool of laughter.

"Gotcha!" He poked my shoulder.

I had to laugh with him, though chilly bubbles still percolated through me. He laughed a little too hard, with just a trace of horror movie.

"So, where are you from?" I asked him.

"DC. I'm on my way home."

"Vacationing in Oakland? Enjoying Jack London Square?"

His demeanor darkened again. "I was on a case."

"Oh. What do you do?"

"How about you? Where are you from?"

"I live in Oakland. Or I used to." A knot clumped in my stomach. I was alone.

"Native Californian?"

"No, I'm a *real* Californian. A real Californian came from somewhere else."

He chuckled. "Where?"

"Erie, Pennsylvania was where I grew up. You?"

"Salt Lake City."

A Mormon I thought, too polite to ask. "Hmm." I returned to my computer. I opened a blank page for my journal. *Just because you're paranoid doesn't mean that someone isn't following you.*

"I'm glad you agree that something needs to be done about the Supreme Court," I said. "Just one guy. Think of how many people are killed in war, or killed because of Johnson's decisions."

"Now it sounds like you intend to do it, to kill Sylvester Johnson."

"Oh, no, no, no. It's fiction!"

"Are you sure?

"Yes."

"Are you sure?!

"Yes!"

Mortified at myself for saying too much, I continued writing for an hour. Deathless prose, or so it seemed to me. Then, despite the caffeine, or maybe because of it, I fell asleep. I woke up to the disembodied voice again. "We'll be landing shortly. Please turn off your electronic devices...etc."

I could see the lights of the city twinkling joyously. The darker moments coming off the caffeine, made me wonder if maybe humans were a cancerous growth on the planet, the cities like tumors sucking the lifeblood from the living earth. No other species in the universe, so far as we know, has embarked on the trajectory that humans are on, call it material culture: cars, cities, toilet paper, TV, guns, iPhones, language. You name its manifestation, it's unique. And maybe it isn't benign. Maybe it's deeply malignant. I shook off these thoughts as plane shook from activating those huge spoilers on the wings to slow us down, ready to crash. But we landed, and despite going far too fast (*what if the brakes fail?*), we managed to slow down and stop at the gate.

My fat friend and I exchanged pleasantries. "Good luck to you in whatever your endeavors are," he said. Was there menace in his look?

"And to you."

There were no hotels under $90 a night on line, so I took the bus from the airport to Union Station, figuring the cheap hotels would be near the train station. Of course Union Station had evolved into an upscale shopping center and much of the neighborhood had been gentrified, but, dragging my large wheelly suitcase, I found a pocket of sleaze about six blocks west, near the homeless shelter. One cut above it, the Hotel Manolo was a crumbling brick building, its high-ceilinged lobby populated with grizzled alcoholics of different races staring into space from faux leather chairs. *Perfect.*

A pimply, cadaverous kid in his early 20s said the rate was $40 per night. *Perfect.* He looked like a Uriah Heep, mean and ugly, but he seemed glad to welcome a guest as upscale as myself. I rode the creaky elevator to the third floor and found my new home, room 303, with a sagging double bed, a pink chenille bedspread, grey carpet stained with undefinable bodily fluids. But it had and a little desk for my computer and its own bathroom, lined with splotches of mildew and the grit of worn-out porcelain. *Perfect.* This is where I always thought I would end up.

3

Hole in the Wall

I woke up the next morning with a throbbing headache and no idea where I was or what I was doing there. I vaguely recalled something about Washington and the Supreme Court, but I couldn't remember if I was here to write a novel about someone arranging the assassination of one of the Justices, or if I was here to arrange that assassination, and the "writing a novel" conceit was just a cover. I took some pills, Vicodin, and concluded that, most likely, I was writing a novel.

Whatever I was researching, checking my phone/calendar, I was reminded that I had a lunch date with my cousin Fred Wallace, six-three, 200 pounds, a Secret Service agent on presidential detail for three successive Vice-Presidents, Al Gore, Dick Chaney, and the first term of Joe Biden. We met outside the Palm Restaurant in Tyson's Corner, McLean, Virginia, a mile from CIA headquarters. Fred was dressed in a dark suit, white shirt with open collar, and Ray-Bans. No trench coat, though fall was crisping the air. It's a good thing we met outside, because about half the lunch diners were dressed the same way, like a spoof of Men In Black, itself a spoof, a spoof of a spoof.

"Fred."

"Peter."

"I haven't seen you since that family reunion about ten years ago."

"You haven't changed a bit." I said.

"You got to have the steak. It's to die for."

The menu said $30. Way over my budget.

"Steak it is. How's your Dad?"

His Dad and I had grown up together near Lake Erie. We were only a year apart, but he was a little strange, which dropped him to the bottom of the pre-adolescent pecking order. I teased him relentlessly like all the kids when we were around them, but when it was just the two of us, we could play "Go Fish," and I could secretly enjoy his company.

"He's good. What are you doing in DC?"

"Doing research for a novel. About the Supreme Court."

"I do remember that you were a writer. Or trying to be. Have you published anything yet?"

"I've written a bunch of novels, all of them pre-published. They are kind of literary, not necessarily mass market. But now I want to do a thriller and tap into the current zeitgeist. Kind of like *The Pelican Brief,* you know? How's things with you?"

"All right, I guess. They've got me on a desk job. Kathy's happy that I'm safer, but I miss being on the front lines."

"What's it like guarding the vice-president?"

"It's intense, because you got to be on high alert

almost all the time. You can't daydream while the VP walks through a crowd. You have to keep your eye out for bad guys, for anything suspicious."

"Does the Secret Service guard the Supreme Court Justices?"

"No, they have their own protection." He raised an eyebrow at me. "Why do you ask?"

"The book."

He gave me a knowing look. "The book." He repeated. My first foray into Washington politics, and already I'd aroused suspicion. "You have a radical reputation, Peter. You're not planning some kind of revolutionary manifesto, are you?"

"No, no. Been there, done that. I'm too old for all that now."

"That's good, because I'd hate to have to report my own cousin as a security risk." He laughed. "What's the story about?"

I hesitated. "It's about a guy who wants to arrange the assassination of a Supreme Court Justice." I dusted off my rehearsed alternative story line, a bald-faced lie. "Because they're about to vote to take away our guns by promoting strict gun control."

"Huh. So you're against gun control now?"

"I've changed, Fred. I think we all get more conservative as we grow older. Plus, I'm trying to get righteously published and make a lot of money."

"Huh." He looked at me skeptically. I tried not to avert my eyes. I'm a terrible liar. "They have their own police force. It's not very strong. When they're ruling on a major case, the federal marshals help."

"Thanks for that, Fred." I was honestly grateful that he swallowed my alternative story line. I smiled. "How is Kathy doing? And the kids?"

It wasn't smart on my part to try to get information from people who knew my reputation. I tend to shoot myself in the foot. This operation was too delicate for me to make such mistakes. But I pushed it one more time.

"Is there a place where disgruntled CIA types hang out?"

He looked at me suspiciously. "There is. It's not too far from here, in McLean. It's called the Hole in the Wall. It's in a strip mall off Center Street. McLean is an upscale community, to say the least, but it has its sleazy side. Between McLean Nails and McLeaner's, clever name for a dry cleaner's, huh. I can't go there with you, though."

"How come?"

"Well, I hate to say this, but we're a little like street gangs around here with our agencies. This joint is ex-CIA. Secret Service, FBI, NSA – not welcome. More than not welcome. They usually don't kill each other, but they come way too close for my taste."

"Hey, thanks for the tip, Fred."

"No problem. Welcome back to the United States. Glad to help if it's going to allow people to keep their guns. Some law enforcement types are actually for gun control, but most of us feel safer if the good guys, the honest citizenry, are armed and can help us."

I took a Lyft the ten blocks or so to the Hole in the Wall, which was indeed a hole, dark, dank, reeking of stale beer and urine. A pool table. An ordinary neighborhood bar the likes of which served the vast alcoholic population throughout the country. The walls were paneled with dark fake wood, and festooned with intermittent pots of fake ivy. It was, from the odor, clearly one of those bars that ignored the municipal code banning smoking.

I knew that I had best get used to the atmosphere. I was going to be hanging out here for a while. I figured I would sit at the bar most of the day nursing one or two beers, get to know the bartender and the regulars. Sooner or later, I'd meet somebody who knew someone. Who would give me the information I needed for my novel, I had to keep reminding myself.

Sitting in a bar like this, I could get pretty bored. When I get bored, I get careless. I started talking to the bartender, a slovenly man with a big grey beard and beer belly, long hair, bald at the top like Ben Franklin, dressed in a flannel shirt, Levi's held up by suspenders.

"Is it true a lot of ex-CIA types hang out here?"

"Who the hell are you?"

"Peter Graves. I'm a writer researching a Washington thriller."

"Peter Graves. That sounds familiar. Isn't there somebody famous with that name?"

I hammed: "'Have you ever been in a cockpit before?' 'No Sir, I've never been up in a plane before.'

'Have you ever seen a grown man naked?' The actor. The Airplane movies. Mission Impossible."

"Okay. You actually look like that actor. But we don't like writers here, and we don't like people who ask questions. So consider yourself doubly disliked."

I hoped this was a joke. I know I do look like Graves: ordinary face, good features, bright and bushy white hair – before I shaved it all off. Now I look more like Henry from the old comic book. I laughed.

"I'm serious."

"Okay."

But there was no one else in the bar at 3 PM and the bartender must have been as bored as I was. "People come here to forget. I bought this place so I could forget."

"Forget what?"

"Now they have a fancy term for it. PTSD. It's not just for soldiers any more. People who've done things they're not necessarily proud of."

"Like what?"

"Like killing nosy writers before they learn what really goes on in this town." He wasn't smiling.

"Ha ha." I bravely or foolishly pushed on. "Have you killed a lot of people?"

"Enough so that one more wouldn't make a significant difference."

"Ha ha." Better to back off and nurse my beer. I was prepared to die for this cause, but I wasn't prepared to fear for my life. Especially not before I had accomplished my mission. I tried a different tack.

"I'm afraid they're trying to take away our guns."

"You have a lot of guns?"

I wished I had done more research. "A lot. A .45 automatic from World War I. An Uzi that hasn't been emasculated. A Baryshnikov."

He raised his eyebrow at me. "Kalashnikov?"

"Yeah, who can pronounce these Russian names? An AK-47."

He looked at me with deep skepticism. I decided it might be best for me to shut up. I didn't talk to anyone else the whole day, thinking I would keep coming back until I seemed to be part of the decor. I was also afraid of shooting myself in the foot again. I really wasn't cut out for this job. Didn't they call that the Peter Principle? It's probably named after me. But someone had to do it.

When I got back to the Hotel Manolo, I googled "Who guards the Supreme Court Justices?" The hotel had no Wi-Fi, so I had to use the hotspot on my iPhone. Probably not the most secure arrangement in the world. If I wasn't so lazy, I would have at least gone to the library so my searches could be anonymous. A New York Times article came up, headlined: "Justices Sit on Highest Court, but Still Live without Top Security." Promising.

The next afternoon, I returned by the Metro to the Hole in the Wall. It was later than last time and there were a few more patrons. I brought my laptop and some books I was reading about the Supreme Court. Sylvester Johnson's memoir. I wanted to learn his habits, his passions, his hobbies. Where would he go to let his hair – and his guard – down?

He loved sailing, had a beautiful Pearson 44, a motor-sailor that he liked to sail on the Chesapeake. There were pictures of the yacht, named *Supremacy*, with Johnson at the helm, grinning like a teenager who had just got laid for the first time. Could someone stow away on his boat? Someone with a gun?

A man sat next to me at the bar, nodded a greeting. Young, slender, not nearly so degenerate looking as the other denizens of the Hole. His face had a Middle Eastern cast to it. He was dressed preppy in pressed chinos and a laundered blue oxford button down shirt. He wore slender, stylish sunglasses.

He glanced at my book. "Reading up on Johnson?" He had no accent, which is to say he had an American Middle Western accent.

"Mmm," I said, noncommittally, reluctant to engage, particularly around this issue.

"Kind of a prick, isn't he?"

"Mmm."

"I never understood how a Black man could become such a fascist. He owes his whole career to affirmative action, and then he attacks it."

"I believe that Black people have just as much right to be assholes as anyone else."

"Yeah, I think it says that in the Constitution. So what ex are you? CIA? NSA? FBI? DIA? DEA B-613?"

"B-613? I thought that was a made-up agency from *Scandal.*"

"It is. I was just being funny."

"None of the above. I was in Nam, though."

"Yeah? Doing what?"

"Infantry."

"You saw action?"

"Some." In reality, I had joined the army to oppose the war and spent most of it in the brig for distributing leaflets supporting Ho Chi Minh and the NLF. But I wasn't about to tell him that.

"I was in the CIA. Twelve years. Worked with the DEA on drug interdiction. Got caught acquisitioning a kilo of cocaine for myself. Now I do private security. Blackwater, shit like that. Tariq Shareef." He held out his hand for me to shake.

"Peter Graves." I shook his hand.

"So what're you doing hanging out here? Whatcha looking for?"

"Nothing. Writing a novel about the assassination of a Supreme Court Justice."

"Really? A writer! Wow. I'm impressed."

I figured the guy was probably going to try setting me up for some kind of sting, but avoiding risk wasn't my strong suit. "Do you know anybody?"

"Anybody what?"

"Anybody who would know how to hire an assassin for a Supreme Court Justice."

He cocked his eyes at me. "No. I got caught with drugs, I don't go in for that shoot 'em up stuff. Stick around here though and you'll meet someone."

"Okay."

He looked at me hard. "There is someone. Google 'Aletha disgruntled CIA.' She's out there public and doesn't give a shit. She may well know someone who knows someone who knows someone..."

"Thanks, man. I'll try that."

"Be careful, now. I hear she's a bit of a ball-buster."

"Really?"

"Really."

4

Aletha

Back at the Manolo that night I googled "Aletha disgruntled CIA."

The blog of a young Black woman came up, a woman who'd been ferreted off to a mental hospital for complaining about being sexually harassed during her CIA training. I emailed her: "I'd like to meet you to discuss a project I'm working on." I hoped that was sufficiently vague, as this woman's email was certainly monitored.

She responded right away. "Meet me at the Martin Luther King Memorial tomorrow at 11 am. You'll know who I am by my picture."

It was November, but still warm in this Southern city. Bright, with a touch of oppressive humidity. Sweat failed to evaporate. I arrived by bus at the Memorial at 10:50, time enough to ponder the stillness of the great man, read his quotes. Killed trying to save the nation as no doubt I would be as well. I looked around for suspicious types – certainly a woman like this would be shadowed, if she wasn't a decoy to flush out the likes of me.

I finally spotted her about 11:30, slender, darkskinned, wild cork screw hair with blond streaks in it – just the kind of woman who'd normally get my juices flowing – but the intensity of my focus on the task at hand had subdued my juice-flow.

We sat on the steps and talked – or rather she talked a mile a minute, rattling on about her story of how her superior officer and trainer had tried to seduce her, no, rape her really, and when she complained, they shipped her off to a mental hospital. She was suing the CIA.

I could see why they thought she was crazy – not because of her accusations, but her squirrely manner, darting eyes, constant blabber.

Finally, she asked me: "How did you find me?"

"Some guy at the Hole in the Wall suggested I contact you."

"That funky place full of redneck traitors? I never go there."

"He told me to google 'Aletha disgruntled CIA.'"

She laughed. "Okay. What's your project?"

"Are you sure I can trust you?" I asked. "How can I be sure you're not trying to flush out terrorists with your very public web presence? Do you think you were followed?"

"Now don't get all paranoid, Mr...."

"Peter."

"Mr. Peter. Aletha Maxwell." We shook hands. "They do monitor my emails and tap my phone. But they trained me in how to lose a tail, so they haven't been able to follow me. Besides, they know where we are by the email."

"Well, I'm doing research for a novel I'm writing about the assassination of a Supreme Court justice."

"You're a writer, huh? Cool. Have I read any of your books?"

"No. They're...pre-published."

"What do you want with me?"

"The guy said maybe you could help me with the research. For instance, if my fictional character wanted to hire someone, someone like a disgruntled CIA agent to do this assassination, how could he meet one?"

"Whoa. I'm disgruntled, but I'm still loyal to my country. I don't hang with any of the traitorous terrorist types, if that's what you're looking for."

"It's just a story."

"Which one would you kill, anyway?"

"It's fiction, Aletha. The justice would be a made-up person, based on Sylvester Johnson."

A proud Black woman, she turned white. "Sylvester Johnson? Really?"

"It's fiction, Aletha."

She suddenly got seriously nervous. "Johnson," she said, looking at me with her quizzical green eyes. "Sylvester Johnson."

"You know him?"

"Know him? Of course not. I know who he is. But know him personally? How could that ever happen, Peter? Think about it. Me? Of course not."

I looked back at her as her eyes darted.

"Well, it doesn't sound like you can help me."

"No, probably not. If I hear about something, I could give you a call."

I gave her my card. Peter Graves, Writer.

She looked at the card, then at me. "Peter Graves. How do I know that name?"

"'Have you ever been in a cockpit before?' 'No Sir, I've never been up in a plane before.' 'Have you ever seen a grown man naked?' The actor. The Airplane movies. Mission Impossible."

That evening I googled "Visiting the Supreme Court." I checked to see if the court was in session. I was amazed to find how rarely it actually was in session, an average of eight days a month with only three or four being oral arguments open to the public. You have to line up early in the morning if you want to hear them.

I knew this was the case I was looking for, *Williams v. Florida*. There was a lot of interest in the case, especially from the movement against mass incarceration which was trying to expand voting rights to current felons.

I arrived at the court building in the freezing rain – a cold snap had suddenly hit the capitol – before sunrise. There was already a long line, as well as a small demonstration. I picked up some flyers from the local groups organizing for prisoners' rights.

Coming from California, I wasn't prepared – light khaki jacket, no hat, no umbrella. I was freezing my ass off.

At 7:30, one of the cops handed out red numbered cards, fifty in all. I scored number 49. The metal detector got me wondering if there was technology yet to 3-D print a gun with no metal parts. They herded us to the cafeteria – two eggs over easy and a biscuit for under three bucks. They made us wait some more.

At 9 o'clock, they had us line up by number downstairs from the courtroom. We were led upstairs to lockers where we paid our quarters to store our cell phones, and everything else but the pad of paper and pen we were allowed to keep.

Then they herded us into the courtroom with its grand marble Corinthian columns. I remembered they were Corinthian from the swirls at the top, seventh grade Social Studies.

I sat in the back, on an uncomfortable bent-wood chair. In the front of the room, fenced off from us under the Honduras mahogany bench behind which the justices would sit, were the lawyers and other dignitaries, plaintiffs on one side, defense on the other.

At precisely 10 AM, one of the marshals bade us to stand and chanted: "The Honorable, the Chief Justice and the Associate Justices of the Supreme Court of the United States. Oyez! Oyez! Oyez! All persons having business before the Honorable, the Supreme Court of the United States, are admonished to draw near and give their attention, for the Court is now sitting. God save the United States and this Honorable Court!"

The nine black-robed justices stepped through the heavy burgundy drapes and took their seats. Sylvester

Johnson was seated second from the end of the row, to my left. He looked bored already, like he might fall asleep at any moment.

I imagined pulling out my plastic AK and shooting him between the eyes. I imagined the marshals drawing their weapons and peppering me with a comforting barrage of lead, my last meal before settling into a peaceful, eternal sleep. Too bad I didn't trust myself to do the deed.

The arguments in the case itself droned on, with much excruciatingly boring blank spaces between them. I started to have feverish chills from being out in the freezing rain so long.

The Attorney General of Florida, a bald white man, argued amid repeated interruptions by the justices, that people who commit any crime, whether misdemeanor or felony, should not be allowed to determine who should govern the rest of us. They were willing to be generous in allowing people with one minor offense to still vote, but two offenses made one a repeat offender forfeiting the rights of citizenship. If we can take away their freedom by incarcerating them, surely we can take away their right to vote. This was clearly permitted by the Thirteenth Amendment abolishing slavery: "**Section 1.** Neither slavery nor involuntary servitude, **except as a punishment for crime whereof the party shall have been duly convicted**, shall exist within the United States, or any place subject to their jurisdiction." [Emphasis his.] He continued: "Except as punishment for a

crime. Surely, if such persons can be enslaved, a practice which we don't condone, they can be deprived of
their right to vote."

Is that really what the amendment said? I wished
I had my phone so I could Wikipedia it. I was feeling sicker by the minute, alternately burning up and
freezing, trembling so much people seated near me in
the courtroom were starting to stare. All that chemo
had weakened my immune system.

Then came the attorney for the ACLU, a young
blond woman, who argued that everyone, even convicted felons, deserved the right to vote. She quoted
Michelle Alexander's, *The New Jim Crow*, which argues
that "criminals," predominantly men of color, are the
new caste, the new scapegoat against which discrimination of all types was legal, even if they'd served their
time. She quoted the statistic that in 1970, there were
300,000 people in prison; currently 2.5 million.

I was shivering, even delirious with fever as
Johnson spoke out. "Aren't most of the people you're
talking about drug addicts?"

"No!" I shouted, really loud. It just came out of me.

It took fifteen seconds for two marshals – one
tall, one short, both Black – to each grab an arm and
escort me outside, all the way to the front. "We don't
allow such outbursts," the skinny one said politely.
Yes, I had done it again, blown it. A few more mistakes like this and this mission would be aborted.
Though I couldn't afford it, especially since I was sav-
ing money to pay for my hireling, I took a cab back to

my hotel and curled up in bed for three days until the fever broke. I woke up continuously from my recurrent dream of being in solitary back in Nam. The claustrophobia was the most terrifying thing I could imagine. The shakes from the fever and the fear fed into each other. I made a pact with myself that no matter what happened, I would not go to jail again. I would die first.

My cosmic headache returned. I lay down on the bed and squinched my eyes tight shut. My consciousness became unhinged from my body, or at least from my mind. The peephole of my consciousness slipped into the point of view of the cancer cells – imperialists for the viral world. I found myself at a strategy meeting of White Blood Cells, doomed old-school militarists who were losing. They had no angle on cancer.

Maybe I was imagining the whole thing, but what did that even mean? Imagination is the raw stuff out of which we construct our reality as well as our fantasy. It was as real to me as anything that my disembodied voice was negotiating between the Peter Defense Forces (PDF) (including the White Blood Cells, the T-cells, and the newly introduced Stem Cell Army, miniscule, badly in need of reinforcements). It struck me like an asteroid that this space was what was called the astral plane, for where else would astrocytes or astrocytomas hang out?

I spoke to the The Big C (TBC) troops: "What's the hurry? You know you're going to win. Take your time. Enjoy the ride." This didn't touch a nerve. To the PDF, I heard myself saying. "I know you have a lot of experience, White Blood Cells, but it's time to step back and let the Stem Cell Army take the lead." Honestly, my brain was beginning to feel like the underside of a couch which had been occupied by a dozen rats. Little loose cotton balls with a creepy rattyness to them, the definition of "ratty."

The ebb and flow of my consciousness was both an asset and a liability. Like so many things. An asset because it was highly interesting and gave me a benign model of death. A liability because I had no control, my focus was all over the map. If I couldn't focus on defeating TBC, I wouldn't defeat it. Oh, and it further isolated me because there was no way to communicate what was going on with them to anyone. Neither TBC nor the PDF folks spoke English.

On the fourth day, I went back to the Hole in the Wall in the late afternoon for happy hour. It was cold, but the rain had stopped. I wore my down jacket and took the bus. I sat at the bar nursing a beer, tiny sip by tiny sip. The bear of the owner-bartender gave me a quizzical look, less hostile than the last times, but left me alone. I was still too scared to approach anyone.

There were half a dozen men in the place looking relatively normal, playing pool or just sitting alone drinking boilermakers. At least three of them reminded me of clichés of disgruntled vets like the Willem Dafoe character in *Born on the Fourth of July*.

Then who should show up in the doorway but my old friend Aletha Maxwell, with her wild corkscrew hair, tight jeans, silk paisley blouse, creamy-supple tan leather vest. She sat down next to me. The bartender smiled at her and gave me one of those glances men give each other when they approve each other's dates. "The usual?"

"You do know me, Sonny, Long Island Ice Tea." Vodka, rum, tequila, gin and triple sec with sour mix and topped off with cola. She apparently knew how to drink.

"I thought I might find you here." Her look was so penetrating I sucked in my breath.

"And here I am. I thought you never came here."

She ignored me. "I've been checking in for the last few days. Sonny told me you were here a couple of times, asking inappropriate questions."

"I've been sick as a dog. I waited in the rain to get into the Supreme Court hearings. I caught my death."

"I tore up your card, thinking I couldn't help you. But then I thought some more. Your story stuck in my mind. I decided maybe I can."

"What made you change your mind?" I was wary.

"I remembered you saying how your novel was just a story. I'm out of work right now. Maybe I can help you make a better story, more authentic. And if it becomes a best-seller and you become rich and famous..."

I laughed. "Okay." I still didn't trust her, but I figured she might be of some help. If later it turned out she was working for the feds or something – well, I'd be careful. Famous last words.

"Can we get out of this dump?" she asked. "I'm hungry. Take me to dinner, at least."

"Okay. Where?"

"I'll show you."

She grabbed my hand and led me outside. She flagged a cab and ordered the driver to take us to a cozy French bistro, Le Diplomate, downtown. I liked how she took charge, and I would need to figure out how to raise money for my project anyway. Spending what little I had now wouldn't make much difference.

We were seated in a booth with a curved red leather bench that forced our knees to touch. She ordered for us. "*Coq au vin* and *boeuf bourguignon*. We'll share. And a bottle of Château Léoville Barton 2009." $50 for a bottle of wine?

I smiled, bemused at her assertiveness. It might have turned off many men, but not me. Power in women turned me on. Hayseed that I was, the Léoville tasted like two-buck chuck to me.

"Tell me your story so far."

"There's this middle-aged guy with nothing to lose, a radical who hasn't accomplished much in his life in terms of radical change. He gets this idea to hire someone to take down one of the Supreme Court Justices."

Aletha smiled. "And he meets this young Black disgruntled ex-CIA agent, who leads him to the right people to get the deed done?"

"I don't know about that. Maybe."

"Does he have an affair with this young Black disgruntled?" She twinkled at me.

I blushed. "I don't know yet."

She smiled her captivating smile again, and squeezed my hand. For the first time, I noticed her eyes, a brilliant green, a color some Black people associate with devilment.

We exchanged life stories. My time in Nam, solitary confinement. Marriage to a lovely Latina, daughters, addiction to porn. I skipped the cancer – it might turn her off.

She had grown up in DC with Mission Impossible, Charlie's Angels. Hard working parents. Always wanted to be a spy. 34, never married – most men found her too aggressive. She preferred older guys who didn't mind her taking charge.

"Like me."

"Like you."

That penetrating look again melted some resistance inside my belly and gave me an erection. I paid the $139, trying not to squirm. We got in a taxi. There was really no question of where we were going. "Hotel Manolo, please," I said.

The brown brick hotel, lobby filled with old derelicts, was not romantic. Her look said, *Really? This is the best you can do?*

We went straight to passionate kissing in the creaky elevator, rushed to my room and plopped onto sagging mattress, oblivious to the smell of must and old cigarettes.

She slowed it down. "Take your clothes off. Stand by the bed." She inspected my body as if it were a side of beef she was thinking of butchering. She grabbed my balls and examined my penis. She turned me around and squeezed my left butt cheek. Her lips curled in a devious smile. Sitting on the edge of the squeaky bed, she said, "Undress me."

I kneeled before her and removed her black mid-calf boots. The leather vest and silk blouse. I unbuckled her jeans and worked them off. Lace-trimmed burgundy bra and matching bikini panties – delightfully out of character. Off. Off. Her breasts were small and smooth. No Brazilian, no landing strip. She had a nice bush, black and kinky.

"Make love to me."

And I did. She lay back as I touched her all over, lightly. I suckled her breasts. I went down on her pussy with all the expertise I had gleaned from Nina Hartley's video ("How to suck a pussy"). Aletha spasmed. She guided me inside her where I finished within minutes. We cuddled together sweetly as we drifted off to sleep.

5

Second Date

She woke around 2 AM, dressed hurriedly, and slipped out the door with only a quick peck on my cheek. Half-asleep, I realized I had no way to get in touch with her except email. I opened the door naked and called after her. I had nothing to lose here but her.

In the morning, I emailed her: "Thank you for the lovely time, Aletha. When will I see you again?" Like the Mark Zuckerberg character in "Social Network," I obsessively checked for her response. At 4 PM, I Metroed it back to the Hole in the Wall and sat at the bar, hoping against hope she would show up. I brought a notebook to sketch the next steps in my mission.

Money. Where would I get the money to hire someone? In the back of my notebook I listed every cent I was spending. I had started this venture with $10,000 in the bank. I was already down to $9000, and I'd been here a little over a week. My carpenter's union pension and social security totaled $2000 a month – but most of that went to Mariana. My relationship with Aletha would not be cheap. How much for my assassin? I had no clue. I'd ask Aletha next time. If I saw her again. I suppose I could rob banks like some of the loony left tried back in the day. But now the bankers and their minions are sealed behind the thickest plexiglass, penetrable by a powerful IED perhaps, but that would destroy both the tellers and the money.

The next day I strolled down to the Capital Yacht Club on the Potomac where Johnson's memoir said he kept his yacht, *Supremacy*. The gates to the docks were locked of course, so I could only see the boats from a distance, but having grown up around boats on Lake Erie, I knew what a motor-sailor looked like. I found *Supremacy* in less than a half-hour. It was a beautiful boat, in perfect condition. Deep blue fiberglass hull, brass fixtures polished and gleaming. An ideal boat for DC – the motor function could spirit out the Potomac to the Chesapeake, then open onto full sail. It would be three months before the weather would be warm enough for Johnson to go for a cruise.

I could be patient. The only urgency was to complete my project before the *Williams* and the other rulings – at least four months.

Then there was Aletha. I was already losing patience, grieving to think our tryst might have been all I'd ever get.

Leaving the Capital Yacht Club, I had the distinct feeling of being followed. He or she was professional enough not to be detected outright. In fact, there was no evidence – just a highly untrustworthy feeling. I'd had one paranoid episode, ten years after returning from Nam, so I trusted my instincts. *Just because you're paranoid*, and all that.

So I ran. Into the Waterfront Metro Station, took the Green Line east to the Navy Yard, ran across the tracks to take the Green Line west to Enfant Station, where I caught the Silver Line toward McLean. I sat down satisfied that I had learned the transit system well enough to elude my tail.

Back at the Hole, I waited until almost 9. Maybe I had only imagined Aletha. I was noticing some difficulty distinguishing what was happening in my life and what was happening in the novel. I know the astrocytoma was affecting my thinking in strange ways.

I was about to accept the confusion and leave when she came barging in the door. Clad in tight leather pants, black turtleneck with the leather vest. Leather trench coat. "The usual," she barked, and then glanced at me with a look that said: don't ask.

"I've been waiting for you." I felt suddenly high school nervous in her presence.

"Of course you have."

She gulped her Long Island Iced Tea and said, "Let's go!"

I followed her as she flagged a cab. "Manolo Hotel," she said. We sat in silence, a foot apart. She didn't look at me. The mystery of her demeanor made me tense with anticipation and, yes, hard. She had lost all the rapid-fire run-at-the-mouth nervousness of our previous meetings.

Back in my room, the silent treatment continued. She sat on the edge of the bed while I stood before her, positions we had assumed in our previous encounter. She nodded her head, which I took to mean for me to take off my clothes. She continued to look at me side-of-beef appraisingly. Slowly, and with a slight smirk, she brought the pointed toe of her boot to my balls. I was fully erect by now, embarrassed by the superior way she looked at me. She rubbed her boot against me.

Then she kicked me square in the balls. I crumpled over. Ball-buster that guy had called her. I stood back up, she rubbed her boot against me again. Again she kicked. Only her tiny laugh breaking the silence. I stood up. She kicked again.

By twirling her index finger, she instructed me to turn around. She grabbed my arms and secured them behind my back with those nylon FlexiCuffs the cops use for low level offenders.

What the fuck. What have I gotten myself into? I felt helpless. Deliciously helpless. She pushed her boot against my arm to turn me back to face her.

She nodded. I guessed she wanted me to kneel. She grabbed my hair and positioned my head, the toe of her boot in my mouth. She moved it in and out, in and out. Chuckling. Then the heel. And then the other boot. One more stroke and I'd have added another stain to the floor.

She lay down on the bed and rolled to the other side. My aging knees were hurting, so I gingerly crawled into bed next to her. She kicked my side until I fell off the bed. She seemed to go to sleep. I took the hint and curled up on the pissy brown carpet. Naked, cold, hard.

At around 3 AM, she left without a word.

Like a turtle turned on its back, I rolled onto the bed without the use of my arms. I rubbed my groin against the sheets and exploded. It took three minutes more to wriggle out of the nylon cuffs.

I wasn't a complete stranger to such games. I had fantasies – even as an adolescent seeing pictures of the Holocaust, ashamed to be aroused imagining myself a victim. I had tried to get Mariana to spank me early in our marriage, but it repelled her. I thought my feelings were sick, kept them bottled up inside. But somehow Aletha had seen them, and here we were.

After Mariana first caught me watching Femdom porn ten years ago, I started attending Sex Addicts Anonymous meetings in an effort to save the marriage. While I never felt quite at home among the child molesters and compulsive masturbators, taking the twelve steps seemed to help reduce my fantasy life. But I never could get with the Higher Power thing. I made it through step three before dropping out.

When I studied html to learn how to make web pages, my class project was an online church called "The Church of the Cosmic Wink." It had one doctrine: "It seems like there might be something..."

That was as close to agnosticism as I ever got. I was temperamentally an atheist.

Still, I did like to pray. I prayed now. I prayed that I would be able to complete my mission. I prayed that I would be able to resist the wiles of Aletha Maxwell. But I doubted that praying would work, and a large part of me didn't want to resist. Maybe she was my Higher Power...

6

Third Date

I was getting sick of the Hole in the Wall, but Aletha never responded to email so I kept going there, every day. Neither Sonny nor any of the other regulars warmed up to me, even with Aletha, presumably one of their own.

After a few excruciatingly boring days, Tariq turned up again. I was desperate enough for something to happen that I decided to play along. He was probably active FBI, and his beat was this bar, keeping an eye on the disgruntleds – and me.

But I was writing a novel, I reminded my astrocytes. As far as I knew that wasn't a crime, yet.

"Are you getting anywhere?"

"What do you mean?"

"Well, with her, for instance."

"Remember I told you I was a writer? Researching a novel? That's why I'm interested in hiring a professional. Not actually *hiring* one, but learning how one of my fictional characters might go about hiring one."

"Great cover, Peter."

"It's not a cover, Tariq. It's the truth."

"You may have noticed that in DC there isn't one truth. There are a series of truths and most of them are lies."

"That's true in fiction as well."

"Mmm," said Tariq.

"So, how much would it cost to hire a professional?"

"Depends on the target."

I glanced at Johnson's memoir.

"A Supreme Court Justice? Around $50,000. Plus expenses."

"Negotiable?"

"Not very, if your fictional character were to hire a fictional version of me. Now if you found another candidate and got us to bid against each other, you might lower your price. But of course you increase your risk, the more people who know your plan."

"It's fiction, Tariq."

"Right. Well, you let me know if you'd like to go forward."

"It's fiction, Tariq."

"Right."

Of course, I didn't trust this guy any further than I could throw him, but the money figure was in the range I'd guessed. $50,000. Where would I get that kind of money?

I thought about the abolitionist John Brown and the Secret Six. I had written a screenplay about him and his assault on Harper's Ferry, a bold act in 1859, bold enough to precipitate the Civil War, pivotal in the fight against slavery. Brown had only 20 men in his army, but he was financed by a New England cabal of wealthy abolitionists. Where would I find my Secret Six?

Even the prospect of another encounter with Aletha wasn't lifting my spirits – since she might never come back. And where was that going anyway? Only back to the old addictions. A dead end.

I began to miss Mariana fiercely. I stepped out of the bar and called her.

"Hey."

"Hi!" she sounded happy to hear from me. "How's it going?"

"Not so well. I'm missing you."

"Good! Maybe you should give up this project and come home."

"Maybe I should. I miss your smell, the warmth of your touch, your smile."

"Aww."

I teared up some, even sniffled.

"Are you crying?"

"A little."

"You don't have to do this. You can come back to me and live out an ordinary life. You did your bit to try to change the world. Time to relax now. You don't have enough neurons left to enjoy life much longer."

"Was it those imploding astrocytes that made me think I was the one who had to do this thing?"

"Come home, Peter. I love you. I don't think I realized how much I do love you until you went away."

I quoted, "'How can I miss you if you won't go

away.' Okay. I'll get a ticket tomorrow, be back by next week, okay?"

"Really?"

"Really."

"Okay! See you soon then!"

"See you soon!"

I felt a smile warm my whole body as I hung up and let the reality of giving up my stupid mission percolate through me.

Back inside the bar, sitting on a stool next to my stuff was Aletha. How'd she get in without my seeing her?

"Hi." She was smiling.

"Hi!" I had a sinking feeling – glad to see her and sorry to see her at the same time. She was wearing a leather miniskirt, fishnet stockings, her all-too-familiar boots. Leather aviator jacket, silky white see-through blouse. Her silver-dollar nipples shined like moons.

"I've got a treat for you tonight. My apartment." That look again that told me I had absolutely no choice.

We hailed a cab. She gave the driver her address on O Street Northwest and smiled at me alluringly as she squeezed my balls hard. "These are mine, Peter."

"Mmm."

"Say it, Peter."

"Say what?"

She squeezed harder. "Do I have to script you? Say, 'My balls are yours, Aletha.'"

"My balls are yours, Aletha." The driver's shoulders went rigid.

"Good boy." She relaxed her grip, but kept her hand on my – or her – genitals.

"What's this neighborhood?"

"It's called Shaw. They keep trying to gentrify it, but it keeps reverting to hood – classy hood."

Her apartment was in one of the familiar brick row houses that populate DC. Built in the 1910s, the houses look single-family – and once were. But most of them had been chopped up into four units or more. She was on the bottom floor.

I expected the walls to be hung with whips. Instead minimalist, Ikea modern. White walls, paintings by African American artists Jacob Lawrence, Emory Douglas, Caribbean abstractionist Winston Branch. Rattan peacock chair a la Huey P. Newton.

The apartment was tidy except for the bathroom. "You might have to clean that for me." She smiled. The bedroom had burgundy walls and candles everywhere. The double bed, covered with a quilt, was set on stilts.

She sat on the edge and her eyes bid me to stand before her. A nod to remove my clothes. "You're not at the gym. Strip for me, Peter." I hummed "The Stripper," and wriggling my hips, unbuttoned each button, tossed each article to the side.

All of me, naked, stood before her at attention, as did my cock – which she gave a swift kick. I crumpled, stood up again expecting another. She reached under her leather miniskirt and pulled off her violet boy-cut panties with white lace around the legs. "Put these on." I blushed, pulling them up daintily.

"Aw, you're so cute. Come here. Lie down on my lap, Peter." Trembling, I climbed up on her, pre-cum drenching the panties and her fishnet thighs. "Do you know what's next, Peter?"

"I think so."

"What do you think?"

"I think you're going to spank me."

"You're an insightful boy, Peter. Do you want me to spank you, Peter?"

I hesitated. I wasn't sure. Her hand came down hard on my left butt cheek.

"Answer me!"

"I...I do, Ma'am."

"Good boy. But you know, it really doesn't matter if you want me to or not. You know that, right Peter?" She pulled the panties down to my knees.

"Yes, Ma'am."

"Good. You will count to 100."

Whack! "One."

Whack! "Two."

She was skilled, striking a different part of my ass and thighs with each slap. Endorphins trumped the pain. I entered a delirium – "subspace" they called it, an egoless, Zen kind of place.

My consciousness slipped to the astral plane where the battle for my life was taking place. It appeared that the spiky soccer balls of cancer cells were winning, multiplying geometrically. I shivered.

"One hundred."

"Stand up, Peter." I shook off the astral plane. I wobbled, pulling up the violet panties. She giggled. "Oh, you should see that smile on your face. You liked that, didn't you, Peter."

"Yes, Ma'am."

"You're a real pervert, aren't you, Peter?"

"I am, Ma'am."

"You know that was just the beginning, don't you Peter?" Her voice even, hypnotic.

"Yes, Ma'am."

"There's a lot more to come, Peter. A lot more!"

"There's a lot more to come, Ma'am."

"You're not sure what you've gotten yourself into here, are you, Peter?"

"No, Ma'am."

"Too bad, because it's too late now."

"Yes, Ma'am."

"Stand by the mirror. Admire your ass. It's red, isn't it?"

I sidled over to the full-length mirror on the bedroom door and pulled the panties down again. She was right. My ass was red, deeply red.

She chuckled. As I returned to stand in front of her, I caught a glimpse of the inside of her closet door – where the whips and paddles, and floggers, and cat-o-nine-tails, and rattan canes were hung.

"Yes, Peter. Those are all for you. In time. There's no hurry." She opened the drawer of her bed table. Clamps, clips, dildos, and whatnot. She pulled out a long strip of rawhide. She lowered my panties to my thighs. She tied my erect cock and balls, tight.

"Kneel, Peter." Out of the same drawer she pulled a dog collar, pink and studded with rhinestones. "This is a symbol of your submission to me, Peter." She fastened the collar around my neck.

"From now on, you will do whatever I say. Spread-eagle yourself on the bed." She pulled a strap from under each of the four corners of the mattress. She attached leather cuffs to the straps and then to my wrists and ankles. She stood back to admire her handiwork.

I started to tremble with panic, sweating. She chuckled again. "I'm sorry, Ma'am. I...I'm not comfortable. I was in the hole for a year in Nam. I have some issues with claustrophobia."

"Oh, dear," she said, her voice dripping with sarcasm. "And I forgot to give you a safe word like all the manuals instruct. I'm sorry, Peter, there is no safe word. You'll just have to get over your hang-up." She left the room for me to simmer in my own salty broth. Five minutes. Ten.

"Smile," she burst in, her phone/camera flashing. "I'm documenting your journey, Peter. I'm sure these pictures will come in handy at some point."

"No!" My anger flared. "I didn't say you could take pictures."

"Really, Peter? You hardly seem to be in a position to object. Don't worry, we're a team. Trust me. Not that you have a choice."

She sat next to me on the bed. "Can we talk about the book?" she asked.

"Now?"

"Now, Peter. I get why assassinating one of the right-wing Supreme Court justices makes sense – the country is going to hell on a sled thanks to the court. Of course it's always been hell for Black folks. Tell me again, which one do you want killed? I mean which one does your *hero* want killed?"

It was weird to be talking about this, but I was in this position in order to fulfill my mission. "The Black one."

She bristled up. "See how you are? It's always the Black one, even for you so-called progressives. Why the Black one, Peter? There are four other justices who are equally reactionary."

"A lot of Black people hate other Blacks who they see as traitors to the race. I don't feel that way, but it makes for a better story. Meatier, more complex, more nuanced, you know? A white progressive killing a Black man. That's one thing. Another thing is that you may recall Johnson almost didn't get confirmed because there were reports he wasn't very nice to women."

Aletha grunted.

"I know as a white man that I'm steeped in racism, I get that. It comes to us with our mother's milk. All white people in the U. S. are racist because we have tolerated racism for 350 years."

"That's true, Peter. It's to your credit that you admit this. And you need to be...*punished* for it."

"Still another reason is that if we could just get rid of the bad Black justice, the President would try to appoint another reactionary Black person to what seems to be the single dedicated Black seat on the Court, but the Senate wouldn't confirm him and we would have a 4-4 split on the court for the foreseeable future, which favors progressive causes.

"That part makes some sense, Peter. You sure this is fiction?"

"Yes, yes, yes. Fiction, Aletha. I'm not a killer at heart – I was raised Quaker. I could have been a conscientious objector but I decided to join the army and organize against the war from the inside. I talked a lot about Ho Chi Minh as the Vietnamese George Washington. When some friends and I circulated a newsletter supporting his National Liberation Front, I spent the rest of the war in the brig, organizing my fellow prisoners. Not that effective, though – few of them were allowed back in the infantry where they could organize the other grunts.

"I distanced myself from the commies in the late '70s when the movement began to eat itself alive and the USSR, China, and Vietnam seemed to be embracing capitalism. I still think the future of the world depends on people sharing the wealth of the planet. But now it seems the future of the planet is being held hostage by one man. One Justice. Of this Supreme Court."

"You're deeper than I thought. I underestimated you, Peter."

Her look was almost sincere affection.

"Now I'm going to sit on your face. I'm going to smother you with my ass, Peter, and you had better pleasure me, or...who knows? I'm sure I'll think of something."

She climbed on top of me, lifted her miniskirt, and wiggled her ass and pussy inches above my face. I enjoyed the view until she sat with my nose in her ass and her pussy in my mouth. I couldn't breathe. She lifted herself so I could gasp for air, then she sat again, rubbing against my face. My cramped tongue coursed all around her labia, her clitoris, and her ass. I prayed she would come soon. It took a while, but she was glorious with undulating waves and groans. Forgetting to let me breathe. Finally, she climbed off.

"Good job, Peter. I'm feeling generous. I'm going to let you come in your panties. When I count to ten you will spurt, Peter. Understand?"

"Yes, Ma'am."

Counting, she ever so gently stroked my cock and balls through the silky panties. "One...two...three..." And, as she commanded, I spurted my juices into my panties on the count of ten. She smiled at me. "Good boy."

Without another word, she unfastened my restraints. "You'll sleep under the bed tonight." She lifted the bed skirt to reveal a cage about 5 feet by 3 feet by 2 feet.

"Really?" I said, stepping out of the role she'd designed for me, to balk at another bout of claustrophobia.

She was clearly displeased. "Really. Don't be cheeky, Peter. It turns me off."

I wanted my normal life back. Such as it was. I remembered my promise to Mariana. I remembered too that Aletha's photos could make things dicey between me and Mariana, between me and our girls. I crawled under the bed. A one-inch foam pad on the bottom somewhat cushioned my backside. I curled into a semi-fetal position and immediately went into a cold sweat, which lasted most of the sleepless night.

At seven she woke me, all sweetness. "Did you sleep well, Sweetie?"

"No."

"Aw, sorry."

I took a quick shower and dressed, eager to be on my way. My mouth was filled with bile flavored hatred. Toward Aletha and toward myself as for succumbing so readily to her wiles. As I was just about out the door, she said, "There's eggs and bacon in the fridge, bread in the freezer for toast. I like my eggs over-easy, but still runny. Coffee's in the cabinet above the sink. You'll have to grind it first. And don't make a mess, okay?"

"I really should be going, Aletha."

Cold stare. "There's an apron hanging on the back of the door."

I was hungry. Eggs, bacon, and coffee sounded good. I donned the apron, which was full and white, with a 5-inch ruffle around the skirt and shoulders. I felt ridiculous, but I supposed that was the point, since I also felt aroused. Except now I even hated my own arousal.

I cooked efficiently, leaving no mess (unusual for me). We ate in silence. I finished quickly and started to leave again, but she didn't even need to look at me to tell me I needed clean the kitchen first. I did so.

I hung up the apron. "Okay. May I go now?" My humility sounded absurd.

"Yes, dear," she said sweetly. She kissed me on the cheek and playfully slapped my butt as I slipped out the door and greeted the sunny morning with a manic sense of freedom.

7

Blackmail

I knew what I had to do. I rushed back to my room on the Metro, changed clothes, and looked for a meeting on the internet. There was one at noon at a nearby hospital. Though I'm not a jogger – in fact I'm allergic to exercise – I jogged to the meeting.

"I'm Peter, and I'm a sex addict."

When it was my turn, I said, "I've been to a lot of these meetings before, some years ago when I was living out west. I made real progress, got almost through Step 3, where you turn over your will and life to a Higher Power. I couldn't find mine. I looked everywhere, under the bed, inside some churches, but the world just seemed too fucked up to be anything but out of control. Like me. Still, I was able to curb my most compulsive kinky behaviors. Until now. I'm alone in DC and totally caught in a compulsive relationship with a woman who I know is bad for me, but I'm totally powerless to do anything about it."

It helped to admit my powerlessness. I strode out of the meeting resolved to return to California, to Mariana, to normality.

I returned to my squalid room, eager to catch up on sleep. She called my cell.

"We're going to do this thing, Peter. You need to rent a car. Park in front of the Supreme Court building. He should come out about five, driving himself in a black Mercedes, his driver riding shotgun. Follow him. Track his movements. But don't let him see you."

"Do what thing, Aletha? I think you're confused. I was writing a novel, remember?"

"Don't be naïve, Peter. I know what you want. I want to help you."

"Really?"

Silence. "Don't use that tone with me, Peter."

I trudged unhappily to the Rent-a-Car office, asking myself, *why am I doing this?* I can just go to the airport now and get the hell out of here. So what if she sends the pictures to Mariana – it's not like Mariana is unaware of my peccadilloes. Lupe and Marisol are both adults. Maybe they could handle it. Maybe not. Who knows what they're into? S and M had become practically mainstream in the past few years, with the women's magazines that I furtively read in the supermarket check-out line telling us how spanking games and power exchange can enhance our sex lives. Some of us. Not Mariana.

When I dropped out of college for a year, I developed a theory about what I called "the unconscience," that irresistible force that made us do precisely what our conscience tells us not to do. Addiction was a big part of it – alcohol, weed, acid, speed, sex – at the time, but there was something more to it as well, something spiritual. On the level of the goddamn apple in the garden. I was bumming around the country, and there was something about undermining myself, shooting myself in the foot, embracing failure because success raised the standards of expectation to unsustainable levels, replete with stress.

So I watched myself, as if from outside my body, doing what I knew was wrong: renting a car and parking behind the Supreme Court Building on 2nd Street where the underground parking lot entrance was located. According to his memoir, Johnson was the only one with a Mercedes, or any non-American car. Most of the rest of the Justices rode in your standard Lincoln limo. I parked at 3 PM, expecting the exodus from the lot to begin around 4:30 or 5:00. The SCOTUS did not work late.

I re-read the beginning of Johnson's memoir while I waited.

> I came from a long line of lawyers. I wasn't born poor. In fact, our family was one of the wealthiest Black families in Texas. I experienced plenty of discrimination from whites, but it never bothered me much because we had more than any of them. Our wealth, such as it was, was resented by Blacks and whites alike, much more so than if we were white. For some reason, poor whites don't resent rich whites all that much, at least most don't. And poor Blacks don't resent rich whites either, not sure why

that is, not sure why there isn't much more hatred of white folks by poor Black folks. Perhaps it's just our loving nature, or perhaps we're afraid that if we unleashed the hatred we fully deserved to feel, it would consume us, force us to act out against whites in the kind of violent ways that would get us killed in no time. So we pray.

I suppose the question everyone wants to know is how did I become a conservative Republican. It's a fair question, since 95% of Blacks, even the few rich ones, are liberal Democrats. The perception is, especially through the Civil Rights Movement, that the Federal Government under the Democrats helped end the most egregious aspects of discrimination. And segregation – except that many of us were better off before segregation ended. The end of segregated schools caused the firing of countless Black teachers throughout the South, for instance. The law of unintended consequences is one reason I began to think that less government intervention might be better for us.

Many people think that it was pure opportunism that caused me to become a Republican, a political niche that would reward me handsomely in terms of both money and power. But that wasn't the case. I decided to ally myself with the Republicans for the same reason that many if not most Blacks prefer the blatant overt racism of Southern whites to the subtle, insidious, back-stabbing racism of Northern whites. Republican racism is out there front and center for all to see; Democratic racism is more hidden, but every bit as virulent. I value honesty.

When President Lyndon Johnson addressed the troops in Vietnam at the height of the war, he said: "They want what we got, and we're not going to give it to them." Johnson may have been a Democrat, but he had a streak of Southern honesty.

It disturbed me some that I liked the guy. I wanted to hate him – it would make my mission so much easier. His politics were egregiously wrong-headed, no doubt about that. But really he was just another rich guy who clung to conservative politics as the best way to keep what he had. Selfish? Sure. Short-sighted? Definitely. Narrow-minded? Absolutely. But not evil, or no more evil than millions of Americans with insufficient imagination to grasp what the world could be if self-interest wasn't the driving force, if the driving force was the impetus toward community.

At 4:45 PM, the parking lot began disgorging its contents. Limo after limo streamed out. At 5 o'clock PM, the big black Mercedes poked its distinctive three-pointed star and Black driver into the street. I started my cartoonish Nissan Cube. I followed at a discreet distance. The limo maintained a distinguished speed, almost funereally slow, until we hit the 395 freeway, crossed the Potomac, and headed north on the George Washington Memorial Parkway where we maintained the precise posted speed of 55 miles per hour. The Parkway followed the river for about 10 miles, when we took the Chain Bridge Exit in McLean. We followed Crest Lane until we hit the cul-de-sac at the end, a stone's throw from the river. You could see Johnson's massive red-brick Colonial from the bottom of his driveway, which, not surprisingly, was closed off with an automatic gate. The gate recognized the Mercedes and slid open.

I stopped below his driveway, feeling highly conspicuous. There were no other cars on the road. *What was I doing here?*

I parked for less than 5 minutes contemplating my next move when a McLean police car stopped behind me. *Oh, shit.*

A red-headed, befreckled, baby-faced officer approached my window. "What are you doing here?" he asked sharply. "License and registration please."

"I...I got lost. I'm trying to get to the airport." I gave him my California license and the rental car papers.

"I'm going to write you up a warning. No fine or anything, but folks around here are mighty sensitive about who's rooting around their mansions. So I'd advise you to move along as soon as I'm done here." He returned to his car, presumably checked my license to see if I was a wanted criminal, and wrote me out a warning ticket for parking in a no parking zone, evidence that I had been in the vicinity of Sylvester Johnson's home, evidence I didn't need.

I made a U-turn and headed back to the freeway. I'd completed Aletha's instructions. Now it was time to do what I wanted to do. Checking the GPS on my phone, I drove straight west on Virginia 267 to Dulles Airport. I turned in the Cube at the car rental place, and took the shuttle to the terminal. I figured Southwest to be cheapest, so I stood in line.

My phone beeped with a text. A picture of me, naked but for my violet panties, spread-eagled in bondage. I'd already moved beyond this threat. Go ahead, Aletha, do your worst. Send it to Mariana and whoever else you want. I'm still going home.

The next text read, "We're going to carry out your mission Peter." It had an audio file attached, my own voice, highly edited:

> ...*the assassination of a Supreme Court justice... want to hire someone, someone like a disgruntled CIA agent to do this assassination, how could one meet one?...*
> *Her voice: Which one would you kill, anyway?*
> *My voice: ...Sylvester Johnson*

Wow, I thought. She'd been recording me since the beginning. And she's edited out all the references to writing a novel. What mission is she talking about? Maybe she's like me and can't always tell the difference between the reality of the novel and real life. If she turned this tape into the authorities, I'd be called in for questioning. I could explain that I was writing a novel about this scenario and that she had doctored the tape, but they would wonder why she would do that, and she would deny it. Now there was the warning ticket.

A squishy feeling burbled in my stomach. I knew from the internet that in the S and M community, there were people – men mostly – who actually got off on being blackmailed. I wasn't one of them.

I finally got to the front of the line and asked to purchase a ticket to San Francisco on the next flight.

The ticket agent, a kindly blond woman in her late thirties, told me, "I'm sorry but our flights for the next few days are overbooked. I can put you in First Class. A one-way ticket would be $2200. I'd suggest trying some other airlines."

I sat in one of the waiting areas, checking the on-line ticketing services, Kayak, Cheapo, Priceline. No flight for the next week cheaper than $1500. I called Mariana.

"I'm at the airport, but $1500 is too much. I might as well stay here in DC for a while. Even if I'm not going to do this thing, I'll write a novel about it. I'll continue my research. I have met some interesting people."

"I bet," Mariana said. She was disappointed. I told her I was too. Which was more true than she knew.

Back in the hotel, I collapsed into a fetal position, letting the darkness envelop me. I was tired of playing the lone wolf. I had decidedly mixed feelings about abandoning my mission. Assassinating leaders has rarely led to progressive change – not unless it was accompanied by a massive organizing campaign. Yet every moment in history was different. Sometimes stupendous wars make no positive impact on the life of the people. Sometimes the flapping of a butterfly wing makes all the difference. You do what you can do. If you're rational, which most of us aren't, you assess the situation, evaluate your strengths and weaknesses, and do what you can do.

I could have bought a ticket back to San Francisco for a couple of weeks hence. But if I tried to leave again, Aletha would make good her threat to expose me to the FBI. The mission was really all I had.

I decided to connect with the movement fighting mass incarceration. Many of those involved had been incarcerated themselves, which might be a better pool for finding the professional I was looking for. Better than disgruntled CIA.

I checked the leaflets I'd picked up when I visited the Supreme Court. The most active demonstrators were the Unitarians and the American Friends Service Committee. Safe places to start. I found a meeting of some kind of coalition for the next night at All Souls Unitarian on Harvard Street NW and 16th.

The church was a massive red brick colonial structure. It took a while to find the meeting. A dozen people around a set of four tables pushed together. Two were Black, one Latino, the rest white. It had the familiar sense of a white organization desperately trying to diversify, but not quite reaching the critical mass that would make the people of color feel comfortable. But I was learning to be less judgmental in my middle age – these were good people trying to do good things.

"We want to hold a conference on the issue of ending mass incarceration and deportations," the grey but vibrant chairwoman explained to me.

"A conference?" I asked. *Really, we need another conference?* "Haven't we had a lot of conferences already?"

"There have been a lot of conferences, but they included the wrong people. This conference will be focused on the formerly incarcerated community. It will be in the spring, right before the court hands down its *Williams* decision."

Tough guys, I thought. People who know how to kill people. Maybe gang members. I had a long-term dream of turning street gangs into forces for progress, armies of the poor. Probably not the safest game in town, but I'd already stepped onto the wild side.

"With a march to the Supreme Court building as the conference ends?" I suggested.

After the meeting, I went up to one of the Black men. We introduced ourselves. "Matthew Taylor."

"Peter Graves."

"Peter Graves. Are you famous or something? I know that name."

I hammed: "'We have clearance, Clarence. Roger, Roger. What's our vector, Victor?' Peter Graves, the actor. The Airplane movies. Mission Impossible."

He looked at me, raising an eyebrow. "You do kind of look like him."

"Where did you say you worked, Matthew?"

"I work with street gangs."

"We need to talk."

He gave me his card. I gave him mine: Peter Graves, Writer.

We met for lunch in the Capital Hill neighborhood a few days later at the Starbucks by the New Market Metro Station. He was a handsome man, medium length natural, greying around the temples. A few extra pounds. Freckles.

"I was in the Panthers back in the day," Matthew began. "A kid, maybe 12 years old. Their leather jackets and berets, to say nothing of their guns, impressed the hell out of me. That picture of Huey and Bobby and them with their rifles on the steps of the state capitol in Sacramento? That electrified me, us. In retrospect, I wonder if that might have been just a wee bit provocative, but shit, it put the Panthers on the map."

I established my credentials: "What were we thinking? Did we really think we could defeat the war machine? I joined the army to organize from within, but I spent most of the time in the brig."

"Wild time, huh. We really thought we could make a difference. Then the FBI came in with their COINTELPRO, killing most of our leaders. And the CIA came in with their crack cocaine. You read the book, right, *Dark Alliance*?"

"Yeah," I said. "Gary Webb. Committed suicide, supposedly, by shooting himself in the head – twice! Do you have any idea how hard that is to do? I thought for a minute I would investigate his death, write a book about it. I even wondered for a hot minute why no one else was doing it. I wasn't ready to die yet."

"And now you are?" *Was it that obvious? Was it written all over my face?*

"Something has to be done," I said.

"This conference is something."

"Is it?" I was unsure, more concerned that being involved would subject me to more scrutiny than my mission needed. I wasn't about to tell Matthew what I was up to, and the "writing a novel" cover wasn't flying with people in DC. But connecting with him was a powerful antidote to my debilitating isolation.

"I think it could make a big difference," Matthew continued. "People are hungry for a movement right now. Young people especially. They're getting shafted, even whites – PhD's working at Starbucks?" He nodded toward the overeducated baristas behind the counter.

"Forgive my cynicism, but we get them to confer – then what? More occupy?" I asked.

"Occupy was good, the 99%. That's good. That's an accurate class position. That they seemed allergic to the idea of strategy was simply a reaction to the piss poor strategies put forward by the previous generation of activists. Armed revolution. In the United States? Give me a break."

"So now we have conferences."

"And marches, and demonstrations, and voter registration campaigns. These got us pretty far in the sixties."

"Mass incarceration. This right-wing Court is pushing us back to 'go.' What about the gangs you work with?" I asked.

"You think you're cynical. There are some smart guys running the gangs. But let's face it, they're as capitalist as Goldman Sachs. We manage to save a few from careers in crime, but politics taste rancid to them. All they want is a good job, a hot wife, and quiet kids."

"Primitive accumulation. The foundation of capitalism, you're right. Every group seems to go through that phase. Rapacious European colonizers doing slavery and genocide of Native peoples made room for the Italians with their mafia. And the Irish as cops and bootleggers. But Blacks? Totally denied access to capital."

"This isn't news to me, Peter."

"Yeah, but the gangs have the organizing skills. And weapons."

"It's not like no one's tried. From the Panthers on down. Tupac, Public Enemy. You have a strategy?"

"Not really. I have some ideas." I couldn't stop myself. "There's all these cases coming up with the Supreme Court. The use of embryonic stem cells in developing cancer cures, the one I'm most concerned about. The court likes to keep its most controversial cases until the very end of its term. Which is at the end of June. Like school children, the Supremes get the summer off."

"You have cancer?"

"Acute astrocytoma, little tumors in the brain. It skews my thinking occasionally."

"Must be a drag. I'm aware of all these cases, except the stem cell one. June makes perfect timing for a conference. We can combine all the movements by then. The pro-choice and environmental movements are already organizing."

"Okay," I said. "You're winning me over. But what then? A bunch of rallies and marches? The right's gotten used to that. In fact, they like nothing more than to snub their noses at the people's movement: 'yeah, you suckers may have the numbers, but we have the power.'"

"What do you have in mind?"

"Something dramatic. The real progress in the Civil Rights Movement didn't happen until the riots scared the shit out of the powers that be."

"The riots and the Panthers."

"The riots and the Panthers," I repeated.

"Ironically, Oakland didn't riot when King was shot," Matthew said. "The Panthers realized that random violence mostly hurt the Black community. The Panthers' control scared the powers more than the riots. So they picked off the leaders, one by one."

"And then brought in the crack. So yes, something dramatic, to change the equation. I'll join the effort to build the movement against mass incarceration, but let's continue to brainstorm about some action that will make this movement different from the defeated ones that came before."

"Deal."

8

SAA

I threw myself into the movement, signed up for the conference program committee to meet the formerly incarcerated and arrange to give them a major role in the leadership. Maybe I'd meet someone with the skills and vision for my mission.

I was distracted away from the Hole in the Wall. After Aletha's heavy handed blackmail attempt, I'd have nothing more to do with her. After a week, a text showed up:

You will come to my house tonight at 8 PM and spend the night. Do not fail me.

I was determined to ignore her. Let her do her worst. Let her show the pictures to Mariana and the girls – I was sure she pulled their contact info off my phone. Let her send the doctored recording to her former bosses at the CIA. I'd come clean to the authorities about my plan to write a novel, accuse Aletha of blackmailing me. I wrote another few pages of the novel, even introduced Aletha as a character.

My cosmic headache returned. I lay down on the bed and watched as the peephole of my consciousness drifted off to the astral plane on the cellular level where the Peter Defense Forces were battling the Big C. The plane was reminiscent of a video game universe, where squadrons of T-cells would make a suicide run at the spikey balls of TBC and the cancer puffed up itself at yet another victory. Like a General watching the battle from a hill in the Napoleonic wars, I tried to encourage the Stem Cell Army with psychic commands to surround the cancer cells, but there just weren't enough Stem Cells. I needed those special ones outlawed by Congress.

As the daylight dimmed and 8 o'clock approached, something else came over me. I looked for the next SAA meeting, but there wasn't one until the next day. I tried a couple of program calls, people from the meeting who'd given me their numbers, just in case. I got two answering machines. It was as if I had left my body, watching myself from a few feet above my head as I showered, dressed, and got on the Metro.

At her door, I watched as humility took over.

"Peter, my pet." Her full length supple leather shirt-dress, buttons neck to hem,

flared to just above her boots

She nodded. I fell to my knees and crawled after her into the apartment. She sat in the Huey Newton chair. I kneeled at her feet. She fastened the pink rhinestone collar around my neck.

"Remove those nasty male clothes, Peter."

No strip show this time.

She took my head in her hands and spoke in a stage whisper three inches from my face. "I know you thought about calling my bluff. I know you were determined to resist my commands. Yet here you are."

"Yes, Ma'am."

"You know you will need to be punished for that. Severely punished."

"Yes, Ma'am."

"Whipped."

"Yes, Ma'am."

"Seriously whipped."

"Yes, Ma'am."

"When I am through whipping you, your ass will look like raw hamburger meat."

"Yes, Ma'am."

"Look at that tiny hard on." She rubbed the toe of her boot against my balls. "These balls, they're mine. Right, pet?"

"Yes, Ma'am."

"I can do anything I want to them, can't I?" Her kick rolled me over on my back. "Anything."

"Yes, Ma'am."

She took my balls in her hand and squeezed them hard. Until I had to suck in my breath. She laughed her evil laugh.

"I could even cut them off."

I said nothing.

She raised her voice. "I could even cut them off, right Peter?"

I still said nothing.

She grunted. "This won't do. Your defiance will not be tolerated. When I do cut them off, and I said when, you

won't be Peter any more, will you? You'll be Peterless!"
She laughed at her own joke. "How's Petunia sound?"
She smiled and stroked my face. "My little Petunia." She
stared lovingly into my eyes. "No, a little too frivolous.
Pamela is better. Pamela you will be.

"Go into the kitchen, Pamela, and get the big
knife in the drawer to the left of the sink. And bring
the sharpening rod, you know, the long pointy steel
thing in the same drawer."

I hesitated.

She kicked me hard in the balls, and I fell over
again.

"Damn, Pamela. You are just setting yourself up
for it, aren't you? You understand that your pain is
my pleasure. For every level of pain you reach, I reach
the same level in pleasure. That's the way it works.
And it's all about my pleasure. Understand?"

"Yes, Ma'am."

"Go get one of those whips in my closet. Any one
you like, from the velvet flogger to the bullwhip.
Damn that one smarts. Did you know the snap of a
bullwhip is caused by the tip of the whip breaking the
sound barrier?"

I crawled into her bedroom and looked at the array
of implements. Velvet floggers as she said. Leather
paddles. Riding crops. Cat o' nine tails. Ping-pong paddle. Razor straps. I chose what I thought would be relatively mild, a rattan cane, a long one with a handle.

When I handed it to Ms. Aletha, she laughed.
"You're a dumb boy, or a dumb whatever you are

about to become. Or a glutton for punishment." Her arm around me, in a sultry stage whisper right in my ear, "Are you a...glutton for punishment, Pamela? I guess we'll find out, won't we? Anyway, Sweetie, you have brought me one of the most painful devices in my closet. Your ass is going to smart." She stroked my thighs with the cane.

"Assume the position, Pamela."

I knew what she meant instinctively. I turned to give her a comfortable shot at my ass. I put my face to the floor and raised my ass to my Superior. I closed my eyes.

Whack.

"Count to ten, Pamela."

"One."

Whack

"Two."

"Look at that, you fucking slut – you still have a hard on." She kicked me in the balls and whacked me again.

"T-t-three."

By five, I was deep in that blissful, egoless sub-space, welcoming each new stroke of the cane. I wiggled my ass girlishly to encourage her. Each blow came harder. The harder the blow, the deeper into the endorphinated bliss I sank.

"Ten."

She stopped. "You should see the marks, Sweetie. Very nice. Each one makes me hotter, first in the making of it, now in the looking at it. Let's go in the bedroom."

I followed her, crawling. "In the bottom drawer of my bureau are my panties. Later you'll buy your own, but for now you will pick seven pairs, one for each day of the week." She slapped my balls sharply with the cane. "And get rid of that hard-on, slut. I don't want your pre-cum dribbling over all my Victoria's Secrets."

I took a deep breath and opened the drawer. There were piles of panties in every style and color – hipsters, bikinis, boy-cuts, briefs, control briefs, thongs, G-strings, and brazilians. I ran my hands all through their slithering silkiness. The stroke of the cane whacked my raw ass. I screamed.

"Stop playing with them, you pervert! Just choose seven and be quick about it because we just getting warmed up tonight, Honey Bear. Tonight, my pretty friend, you are in for it. IN-FOR-IT! You hear that?" She ran her hands over my welts.

I chose one of each style, a deep violet bikini, a lacy fuchsia hipster, a lavender boy-cut, bright red satin briefs, burgundy control briefs, a leopard-skin thong, a sparkly pink g-string.

"One for each day of the week. From now on, you will get rid of your coarse male underwear and wear panties all the time. Oh, and no more standing when you pee, okay? You sit on the pot like a little lady and you wipe your little peenie with toilet paper, okay?"

"Yes, Ma'am." I was truly embarrassed by how turned on I was.

"Pick one for today."

I choose the thong – because it would be the least comfortable in the outside world – stepped daintily into the leg holes.

From her goody drawer, she pulled two pairs of cuffs, fur-lined leather with silver spikes. She attached one each to my wrists and ankles. "On your knees, Pamela. Did you think that was your whipping? Oh, my love – that was just a trailer for the real movie, coming soon to an ass near you."

I knelt face to the floor again. She snapped the cuffs together to lock me in position, right wrist clipped to my right ankle, left to left. She stood back, admiring her work.

She set up her iPhone on a tripod. "Hope you don't mind starring in the movie, Sweetie."

"I do mind," I said.

Whack.

"Smile, you're on Candid Camera! By the way there's a penalty of twenty strokes for defying me again. Oh, and I had asked you to do something. Something about a knife? Well, since you're useless right now, I'll do it myself." She returned from the kitchen with a nine-inch knife with a thin curved blade and a sharpening rod.

"If you weren't so incapacitatedly useless, I'd have you do this." She stroked the knife back and forth along the knife sharpener. "After all, you'll be the beneficiary of this knife's sharpness when I cut your balls off. The sharper the knife, the less painful the procedure. Maybe I'm too kind to you." She embraced me from behind and carefully slid the knife between my balls and my thigh.

Tears erupted and I choked on snot.

"Aw, poor baby! Maybe not tonight. Maybe you can keep them for a little while. We'll leave it to fate. Or to whenever I get the whim. Right, Pamela?"

I was quiet.

Whack.

"Count."

"Eleven."

Whack. "No. One."

"One."

Whack

"Two"

Whack

"How many whacks until you say 'Yes, Ma'am.'"

"Three."

We were up to ten before I said, "Yes, Ma'am."

"Good girl. As a reward for giving me so much pleasure with your pain, I'm going to let you test drive everything in this here closet."

The cat, the crop, the flogger, the paddle, the bull-whip. At least ten strokes with each, I lost count and left my body, transcending to the ceiling to watch the very erotic scene unfold. I was watching myself in the movie she was filming.

When she finally stopped, I was in paradise, tears rushing down my cheeks. I travelled to the astral plane and briefly caught a glimpse of the spikey cancer cells shrinking.

Disrupting my reverie, she pushed me toward the mirror. My ass did look like raw hamburger meat that had been left out on the kitchen counter so long it had turned black. Blood trickled down my thighs.

After stroking my welts, running her fingers lovingly through my hair, even gently squeezing my balls and rubbing my cock, she snapped a leash on my collar and dragged me into the living room like a dog, or more like a master abusing a dog. I was choking and gagging. She positioned me in front of her on her rattan throne, opened the bottom ten buttons on her long leather shirt-dress, and picked up the knife. "Now, Pamela, it's your turn to pleasure me. And you better do it right. I'm holding the knife. You never know when that cruelest of impulses may strike. I would advise you to do your best pussy-licking ever." She buried my face in her slobbering pussy. I wrapped my lips around her vulva and her clit and ever so gently licked and sucked – as if my balls depended on it. It didn't take long for her to reach a writhing tsunami of an orgasm.

I lay with my head in her lap for a long time.

Finally, she spoke. "You have given me great pleasure in enduring your pain. but you don't get to come this time, Pamela. We still have a lot to work to do with your attitude. Crawl under the bed and go to sleep now. Nighty-night. Don't let the bed bugs bite."

Cramped in my cage, my backside burned like a Salem witch. But I slept soundly through the night.

In the morning, she ordered me into the bathroom and smeared my body with Nair, the acrid smell reminiscent of beauty parlors where my mother got her perms. After ten minutes, my whole body was burning. "You can shower now." Hair fell off me in big clumps as the water washed over me.

In only the leopard skin thong and the apron, I cooked bacon and eggs. By 9, she was closing the door behind me. "We're going to fulfill our mission, Pamela, by hook or by crook."

Our mission? What mission is that, exactly? A chill came over me as I realized that Aletha had an agenda, but I didn't know what it was.

"What mission, Aletha?"

"You know."

"No, I don't."

"Yes, you do."

By 10, I was back at the Manolo, still under her spell. Like an automaton, I dragged all the male underwear Mariana had bought out of my suitcase and dumped them in the garbage can by the noisy ice machine down the hall. I replaced them with Aletha's loaners.

My addled brain was being scrambled, as if someone was tossing spaghetti and sauce in my skull. My neurons were prancing an elaborate do-si-do. Like lines in the *I Ching*, yin was flipping to yang, yang to yin.

My peephole of consciousness slipped down to the cellular level, to the astral plane, where I could hang out with the stem cells, the general staff of my Peter Defense Forces (PDF). They were backed up by the rather ineffective white blood cells, which were better equipped to fight off a cold or flu bug, and the T-cells, which were more effective, but few in number. The stem cells were bunched in a tumor-like bubble, so I couldn't make out individual cells because they were shape-shifters. As soon as I isolated one in my mind it changed into something else, going from amorphously amoeba-like to a spikey sphere to a long string of an astrocyte.

Rooting around at the cellular level gave me a headache, so I could only stay a minute.

By noon, I'd returned to what most people would agree is "reality," back at the Unitarian Church in a circle with ten other men and one brave woman. "I'm Peter, and I'm a sex addict."

"Hello, Peter."

During my share, I told the truth. "I'm having a hard time. I'm being blackmailed to act out as someone's sex slave. The trouble is I really like it. I make a strong resolve to resist, but then she texts me and it's like I'm outside my body watching myself do exactly as she says, against my better judgment. I'm trying to get to step one. I'm trying to admit that I'm powerless over addictive sexual behavior – that my life has become unmanageable, as the step says. It's not like she's after money or anything – just control. Absolute control. I can put kinky sex outside my marriage in my Inner Circle, but if I don't keep engaging in it with her, she'll out me to my family, and she's got something on me that could trip the legal system. If she tells the wrong people, I could be arrested – or worse. I'm really stuck."

At the end of the meeting, a soft, most likely gay man in his fifties, pudgy with thinning hair and a warm smile, approached me. "Hi, Peter. I'm Zeke. You sound like you're facing a lot of challenges. I've been there, man. I've been sober for 15 years, but every day I need to decide all over again not to act out. Do you want a sponsor?"

Someone sworn to secrecy and anonymity. That could be useful. "Okay," I said. "I could try this process again."

"You don't sound too confident. But I'll take you where you are, where I was a few years ago. Are you ready to start working on your first step?"

"Maybe. Yes. I'm thinking I'm going to call her bluff, that I'm really not going to see her again no matter what."

"Okay. Why don't you work on your sexual history? Let's meet for coffee in a week."

I spent the next week holed up in my hotel working on my first step and assiduously not-thinking about Aletha. Mercifully, she left me alone as well. I met with Zeke at Starbucks near my hotel. I read him my sexual history:

> When I was four, I had appendicitis. A beautiful nurse took me in the pre-op room and gave me a

most delicious enema. I had my first orgasm. In my adolescence, I rediscovered enemas, and with them considerable shame. I stopped when I got to high school. My sexual addictions from then on mostly involved porn, trekking to the local porn shop to see what taboo they were breaking this week. In my 40s, I discovered all these magazines devoted to enema aficionados.

And I found from the videos and magazines that people who liked enemas also liked other things, like bondage, like whipping. I made increasingly frequent forays to the video arcades.

About a year ago, desperate for sex, I set up a profile on Ok Cupid. I started corresponding with a woman who identified as dominant. She would give me little slutty instructions on a daily basis. We never met in person, though we were headed that way.

But I left my computer on one day, and my wife discovered the email exchange. That's when she moved out of the bedroom and I reached some kind of bottom.

"Thank you for that, Peter," Zeke said. "That took a lot of guts."

"It felt good to get it on paper, to own my peccadilloes."

When I got the next text at 9 o'clock the next morning, I was ready. "Tonight, my house 8 PM."

I texted her back. "I'm not doing this anymore, Aletha. Sorry."

"Really? You know what this means?"

"I do. Do your worst. I'll survive."

There. I called her bluff. I seriously doubted she would carry through with her threats.

But for the next eleven hours, it was all I could do to keep my resolve. Every fiber of my being wanted to text her again: "Just kidding. See you at 8." I resisted, I went to another meeting. I called Zeke and left a message. "Zeke. She wants me. I'm resisting but it's tough. I really want to see her. Damn!"

At 7 PM, I started leaving my body again. I started toward the shower, but I held back. I curled up in a fetal position on my bed and let the minutes tick by until it was too late. At 9 PM, I started to relax. I did it. I'm no longer under her spell. I started feeling really good, my whole body smiling at me. I slept soundly through the night.

At ten the next morning, there was a text from Mariana. "Really, Peter? This is your great mission? To humiliate yourself and me? You disgust me. We're done. Don't contact me anymore. Enjoy your perverted life. Good-bye."

Oh, shit, I thought. She sent the pictures. Guess she wasn't bluffing.

By 11, I had a text from my eldest daughter, Lupe, who was 32. "This is unbelievable. You make me want to throw up."

I spent the morning curled up around the hollow in my belly. Is this what they call the bottom, when your whole family abandons you? And can you blame them? I wanted Mariana now, more than ever. But I'd lost her. I knew her well enough to know that her disgust was final. I wanted to cry badly, but I felt too bad to cry. My life was over.

By noon, Marisol chimed in. "How can you do this to Mom? To us? How long has this been going on? Icky, icky, icky. Stay away from me."

At one o'clock there was a sharp knock at my hotel room door. *Oh shit.* I threw jeans over my red satin briefs, hustled into a t-shirt, and answered the door.

I stared down the barrels of two pistols, held menacingly in two hands each.

Two men in dark suits, white shirts, open collars, ray-bans. Both white. Both bald. One fat, one skinny.

"Peter Graves?"

I nodded.

"You're coming with us."

"Am I under arrest?" I did know my rights.

"Much worse than that."

They forcibly frisked me. They put away their weapons, and with one on each arm, escorted me down the elevator and into a black Crown Victoria. Like Aletha, they cuffed my hands behind me with those nylon FlexiCuffs, covered my head with a black hood, and tied the drawstrings around my neck. In silence, they drove me who knows where, maybe a half hour drive, part streets, part freeway, into what sounded like an underground garage, jostled me into another elevator. When we arrived at our destination, they grabbed my belt, loosened it, and pulled down my pants.

"What have we here?" said the fat one, picking his nose.

"Nice, Peter, real nice," said the skinny one, scratching his balls, "Quite the ladyboy, aren't cha?"

With my jeans around my ankles, they pushed me backwards into a closet and slammed the door. By twisting around with my manacled hands, I determined that it was locked. They left me there to stew in my claustrophobia for what seemed like hours, but I outsmarted them by falling asleep. I wasn't particularly scared. I felt strangely calm in fact – deeply sad, but calm. Sad at having lost everything. Calm because I had nothing left to lose.

After a while, the door opened, and a deep voice ordered me to stand up. My hood was removed, and I saw that it was the same two agents – Thing One and Thing Two I named them. They pulled me out of the closet into the barren room, my pants still at my ankles. They sat me in one of the three chairs around a small metal table in the center and released my wrists. They stared at me.

"Can I pull my pants up?"

They looked at each other and smirked. The skinny one said, "But your panties are so pretty, Peter."

The fat one, Thing One, picking his nose, said, "Okay," and I pulled up my pants.

Scratching his balls, Thing Two, said, "So, you want to assassinate Sylvester Johnson."

"No," I said. "I'm writing a novel about someone who wants to assassinate a Supreme Court Justice.

Aletha doctored the tape so she could blackmail me."

"Aletha. We know all about Aletha."

"What do you know?"

"We know she used to be CIA."

"And what are you guys?"

"Us?" asked Thing Two. "We're nothing. We don't exist. We're off the grid, more anonymous than Anonymous so we don't have to wear masks. Our faces are our masks."

"Really?" I said.

"We think she's working for BlackRiver now. But we don't know who has hired them for what job." They both looked at me expectantly.

"She hasn't told me anything. Just that she was suing the CIA for sexual harassment."

A continuation of the expectant look, turning plaintive, as in *C'mon, Graves, give us something.*

"How would you describe your relationship with her?" asked Thing One in a surprisingly low voice.

I blanked. How would I describe it? To these thugs? "We're...lovers." As I said it I felt an enormous warmth toward her and a longing that can only be described as love. *Shit. I am one sick mother.*

"We can make your life difficult. We can turn the soundbite over to the FBI. They could make quite a sensational case out of it. They might not be able to convict you, but you never know. They'll ruin your life, which is all they want."

I was catching a glimpse of where they were going. And thinking that my life was already ruined.

A deep shadow fell over me and my body temperature dropped 30 degrees. I was thinking of all I had lost with Mariana.

"We want you to wear a wire and ask her what she's up to."

I laughed. "I don't think you understand our relationship. I'm naked when I'm around her. Where would you put a wire? Besides, you guys need evidence? For what? Maybe you watch too much TV."

The two agents looked at each other. Thing Two said, "You have a point about the nakedness. And the evidence. But we do need to know what she's up to. Will you work with us?"

"Do I have a choice?"

"No."

"Okay, then." I was thinking I would get out of here and go straight back to California. Maybe if I talked to Mariana, told her the whole story…

"Good," Thing One continued. "We'll release you then. Don't try anything funny or we'll turn over the tape to the FBI. Report to us by phone every day. This phone." He handed me a flip-phone burner. "Don't contact her. Wait for her to contact you."

They hooded me again and drove me back to the Manolo.

I curled up in a fetal position wrapped around my sorrow, alternately sleeping and plotting my next move.

9

Abduction

For better or worse – most likely worse – I was still under Aletha's spell. After showering, I donned the pink lace bikini panties.

I needed to talk to someone. I called my sponsor, got his answering machine. "I'm working the program," I lied. "Praying, meditating, thinking about step 2."

Tried my cousin Fred, got his answering machine as well. "Some federal agency is hassling me, but I can't tell who they are or what they want. Can you help?"

Matthew actually answered his phone. We made a coffee date.

At Starbucks, we talked about how the conference organizing was going, that we now had endorsements from NOW, EarthFirst, NAACP, different cancer groups.

I gritted my teeth. "All these cases. You know the one thing that would make a difference?"

"A different court?"

"A different court, different by just one vote."

"Hmmm. What are you saying?"

"In your dealings with the gangs, have you met anyone?"

"Anyone what?"

"You know."

"No, I don't, Peter."

"Someone who could handle such a job."

"What sort of job?"

"You know."

"These guys are well protected."

"I know."

"Hmmm." A wry smile came over Matthew's face. As if it was just dawning on him what I was getting at. "Might take some money."

"Yes, it might."

"I don't know, Peter."

"We've both been revolutionaries, right? In those days, we were unconcerned about the numberless deaths it might take. This is just one."

"I don't know, Peter. Those days are gone. I'm not sure I have the stomach for this kind of stuff. Violence breeds violence. But. One guy. I see your point. I'll ask around."

Back at the hotel, I tried to write to Mariana.

I'm so sorry, Babe. So, so sorry. About everything. I'm sorry you got involved with this. Would it help to know that you found out about my latest indiscretions because I called her bluff about blackmailing me? That the only way I could see to get back to you was to be free of her threats? But now, I don't know what's going to happen. Always know that I never stopped loving you and that I want nothing more than to come back to you.

I remember the good times. (God, they were good!). Like when we visited your family in Cuernavaca. We went to the cemetery. The fantastic Mexican cemetery with elaborately sculpted tombstones with pictures of saints and Milagros and dried flowers and shrines indicating many visitors. On the other side was the gringo cemetery, with its even rows of identical headstones shaped like Moses' tablet, protruding from the earth like shark's teeth. How deeply we felt that separation and at the same time our united dazzlement at the Mexican version and the culture that loves its dead so much it must love its living even more.

It was noon by the time I dragged myself out for breakfast. I was planning to walk the three blocks to Denny's to enjoy one of my favorites, the Southwestern Skillet – grilled potatoes, onions, peppers, mushrooms, cheese, and chorizo, topped with two poached eggs.

I made it half a block. A black van screeched. I froze. A Black man jumped out, stuffed my head in another black bag, and threw me roughly in the back. He proceeded to hog-tie me, bending me backwards and tying my wrists to my ankles, as the van raced off. I don't even know if I was afraid at this point, but I do know that I had a hard-on, even as the sweat beads of claustrophobia formed on my forehead.

After a short drive, we entered a street level garage. Two people, from the sound of their shoes, a man and a woman– the click-click of her heels, the clump-clump of his boots – picked me up roughly and carried me downstairs into a space that smelled of mold like a basement.

The click-click woman fastened a collar around my neck and untied me. She pulled down on the leash until I was kneeling. I heard and felt her use a large scissors and cut up the front of my shirt and along the seams of my jeans. The red lace bikini panties did nothing to conceal my throbbing erection. She kicked me in the balls.

Not a word. The bag was still on my head. She pulled me by the leash and stuffed me in a cage just large enough for a big German Shepherd. I heard the footfalls retreat.

I was hungry. And worried about my fate. I waited about an hour. Then I decided to yell. "Help!" I yelled. "Help!"

I heard the heels clicking quickly toward me. Her hands roughly grabbed my head, reached under the black bag, and stuffed a handful of dry kibble in my mouth. Sawdust with a liver taste. Allowing me a minute to chew, she strapped on a ball gag. The cage clicked shut, her heels clicked away.

At least another hour – though the passage of time had ceased to be meaningful. At last the woman pulled me out of the cage and dragged me crawling across the room. She sat in a chair. "Hands!" I held them out. She fastened leather cuffs on my wrists. Using the leash, she turned me so she could reach my ankles, and strapped leather cuffs around them, snapping my right wrist to my right ankle and my left wrist to my left ankle.

"Pamela," the woman stage-whispered as she removed the bag from my head. My eyes focused on Aletha's scowl. "I'm disappointed in you." She looked at me – a little wistfully, I thought. "I'm so disappointed in you." She was wearing a leather mini-dress, fishnet stockings, and her trademark high-heeled boots.

"Mmmffff," I managed through my gag. I was fearful as to what she would do with me now. Her rage seemed limitless. At the same time, I relaxed into the passivity of knowing there was nothing I could do about this situation. I was utterly trapped, eliminating all the stress of decision-making.

She lifted my chin and kissed me passionately on my ball-gagged mouth.

She stepped away. "Pamela, this is Roger. Roger, Pamela." A man stepped out of the shadows and stood next to where she sat. He was wearing those steel-toed worker boots like they sell at Sears, tight leather pants with a conspicuous bulge in the crotch, and no shirt. He had six-pack abs, and a muscular chest – not ostentatious, not jailhouse muscles. His light caramel face was soft. His eyes were kindly, his smile warm. He wore a small gold earring in his left ear. His head was fully shaved, like mine. His chin sported a small Leninist goatee.

"Hello, Pamela," he said in a deep, confident voice. "I've heard a lot about you."

Aletha said, "Roger is going to help with your training. We have agreed that your obedience will be better achieved if you are in chastity. Roger?"

Roger held in his hand a stainless-steel cock cage with electrical wires attached to the top of it. *Yikes!* It was curved like a soft penis, with rings like a spring to surround the shaft and a large ring that locked behind the balls with a small padlock. "This is called a Jail House Chastity Device and will take care of your bothersome hard-ons," Aletha said. "Stand up."

I tried to stand, but with my wrists attached to my ankles, I fell over. Aletha laughed, though not Roger. She unclipped the cuffs and led me by the leash to a large X-shaped St. Andrew's cross, to which she snapped my cuffs so I was spread-eagled, like that famous DaVinci drawing. I could see the whole room – some kind of dungeon with every kind of torture device I had ever thought of: stocks with holes for hands feet and head, medical tables with stirrups, whips, crops, canes, paddles. Gas masks, hoods, a sling chair. All in a room 20 by 20 feet, concrete floor and walls, no windows, a heavy, presumably soundproof door.

"Look at her, Roger! She's so excited. We need you flaccid, Pamela" – she slapped my erection hard – "so we can lock you in. Roger? Will you do the honors?" she asked.

"I'd be delighted." Soft-voiced Roger had a wicked grin.

He stuffed my cock into the cage, locked it, and strapped the whole apparatus around my waist.

"Very nice. Let's demonstrate, shall we?"

Aletha lifted her dress to reveal her panty-less pussy, which she rubbed up against me. With her hands, she stroked my balls. My erection returned with a vengeance accompanied by a sharp electric shock, which would have doubled me over were I not restrained.

They both laughed. "No more hard-ons for you, sissy girl. I also have an app on my iPhone which allows me to send you a charge whenever I feel like it." She flashed her iPhone and pushed an icon. I convulsed. "Thank you, Steve Jobs!"

"By way of introduction, Pamela, Roger's going to whip you now. I know he looks sweet, but looks can be so deceiving. He gets off on whipping white boys, especially white sissy bois. He calls it 'reparations.' He wants to repay your race for all the whippings your people inflicted on our people over the years. You don't mind, do you Pamela?"

The gag blocked my answer. She took me down from the cross and snapped my cuffs to a whipping bench, a wooden construction horse with a leather-covered cross piece about a foot in diameter, stuffed like a sofa. My red panties still hung below my buttocks.

Roger knelt by my head and talked to me in a tender voice. "It's okay, Pamela. It's for your own good.

I know who and what you are. You will enjoy it and I will enjoy it. Yin and yang." He rubbed my buttocks with surprising gentleness. He stroked my scrotum enough to arouse me without triggering the electric cage. Then he slapped my right buttock with his hand. Hard. I grunted. He laughed. He gently stroked some more, then he raised his hand off my left buttock. I gasped, anticipating the blow – which didn't come, and didn't come, and then! My body writhed with surprise. Roger chuckled. The spankings got harder.

As he spanked, he preached. "Maybe this is the only way to beat racism, to beat the shit out of y'all. And, I fully get that it works for you too. You white boys wear your guilt about racism like a sign, 'get away from me.' But (whap!) doing what I'm doing to you does something to equalize the psychological score. We're turning it into play! (Whap!) Some people would say we're trivializing racism by eroticizing it. But this is exactly what we need, to *lighten the fuck up* about racism. (Whap!) In a sense, we're pricking the balloon of racism's self-importance. When we can *play* with racism, we are on the way to defeating it."

He exchanged his hand for a razor strap. "We're not counting Pamela. I won't be satisfied until I've whipped you as many times as your people whipped us as enslaved people. You...we...should live so long." Each blow harder. At around 15 – the point at which I didn't think I could stand the pain – I slipped into selfless, blissful subspace. Each blow sent a surge of endorphins through my body. I felt a great upwelling of love for Roger, who seemed to sense my beatific smile.

My consciousness slipped into the astral plane, as if entering a whole other dimension. Again I saw the cancer cells shrinking and the Peter Defense Forces growing stronger. Aletha and Roger were curing my cancer? Sounded unlikely, too good to be true.

One of the stem cells seemed to morph into a tiny creature, a rodent, who scurried back and forth across the battlefield. *What the fuck?*

The reparations idea worked for me – I tote my burden of white guilt full time. To expiate it by giving pleasure to a man whose people were enslaved for generations allowed waves of guilt to flush out of my body.

Somewhere close to 50 strokes, the unbearable pain returned. I screamed through my gag. I wiggled and writhed in my restraints like having an epileptic fit. My crying became sobbing. The whipping abruptly stopped. But not the deep visceral sobs. After 10 minutes, all was quiet. I could picture the angry red welts on my ass and thighs, felt the trickles of blood from those places where he'd broken skin.

The lights went out. It was as dark as a grave. They slipped my panties back over my cock cage and left me on the bench. What must have been 12 hours felt like days. I had to pee, of course, all over the bench.

I could hear two sets of feet return, one in high heels, one in work boots. Roger removed my gag.

"Look, she soiled her panties," Aletha sneered. "Next time we'll put you in diapers."

Roger wedged my head inside a latex mask. The eye-holes were sealed with removable flaps. He un-snapped my shackles from the bench and helped me stand. They laughed when I couldn't keep my balance. They each took an arm and guided me to a bondage table where I was laid on my back, my arms and ankles strapped down. They left.

When they returned, Aletha stage whispered in my ear. "When we are done with you tonight, you will happily agree to do absolutely anything we demand of you, including giving up your balls."

I said nothing. She slapped my rubber face.

"Yes, Ma'am," I said.

"We are going to remove your access to sensation one modality at a time. We have already taken your sight."

I heard a snort of air like a bicycle pump as my face was squeezed by the mask.

"It's inflatable, your mask. Every time I pump the bulb, I take away another of your senses." Suddenly a balloon of vinyl filled my mouth. I could no longer speak, though I could suck some air in around the edges. Another snort. I could no longer breathe through my nose.

"We can do anything, you know. We're ex-CIA. We can kill you," she said calmly. Another snort. I could no longer hear.

I felt like I would die. My heart was pumping at Zumba speed. With another snort compressing my face, I couldn't breathe at all. Tears flowed. I observed myself leaving my body, a speck of consciousness hovering about this mummified creature. I saw myself back in the hole, in the brig, in Vietnam – a pit dug in the earth. A vertical grave. Even though my nose was sealed, my mind was filled with that dank and moldy smell of earth.

Just as I was on the verge of passing out, a rush of air filled me. They let me breathe for one minute, then took my breath away again. They did this at least five times before I gave up, before I decided I would just die. I settled into the darkness without resistance. There was no light. I was intrigued that in the black hole darkness there was no way to know where I was. Just a speck in the emptiness, the solid emptiness of darkness. Like I was an atom in an unknown molecule, but I knew one thing: that I was.

They deflated the mask. I could hear. I could talk. "Are you ready to surrender, Pamela?" Aletha asked in her kind, sultry whisper. "Or must we continue to squeeze the life out of you."

I hesitated. They started to seal the orifices again. "Wait!" I cried.

"Yes, Pamela?"

"I surrender."

"You'll do anything we say, then?"

"Yes."

She slapped my face. "Yes, what?"

"Yes, Ma'am."

She slapped me again. "And?"

"Yes, Sir."

"Good girl."

I smiled. I felt like a good girl. I felt light. I felt easy. I was dead and yet I was still living. Still experiencing curiosity – the thing I imagine I will miss most when I actually die.

They removed the mask and unstrapped me. They returned me to my German Shepherd cage to sleep. I lost all track of time. I remained deep in subspace, my body a beatific smile. Blissfully egoless, utterly resigned to my fate, without regrets. Only briefly did I enter the astral plane where I saw the rodent scurry. My speck of consciousness started chasing it, like Alice after the white rabbit, but it was too fast and even on that level I was out of breath, Aletha and Roger had taken my breath away.

In what I later learned was the morning, Aletha, in black Lycra Spandex pants and jacket of bicycle racing drag, released me from the cage. Her long, warm hug nearly closed the circuit of my cock cage, but she pulled away just in time. She gave me some clothes nearly identical to hers – black Lycra Spandex compression pants and a skin-tight zipper jacket. She kindly included a pair of black spandex panties. The bulge in my pants from the cock cage made me appear horse-hung, but I was beyond caring what anybody thought.

She looked me over approvingly. "It's hard to find the androgynous clothing you deserve, but these will do for now. Roger and I want you to resume your normal life, such as it was. We trust you. Completely.

Absolutely. Totally." She handed me a black leather fanny pack. "This has your cell phone, money, keys, and stuff. You know we can trigger your cock-cage remotely. We also added a tracking device to your cock cage, so we will know where you are at all times. We know you won't try anything funny. You have a week till your next training. You're almost ready for your mission."

"What mission?" I asked. She'd mentioned this before. *What fucking mission?*

"You know."

"No, I don't."

"Yes, you do. We will summon you. We don't want you to know where this place is, so we will hood you again while we drive you to the Manolo."

"Yes, Ma'am," I was as docile as a puppy dog.

10

Higher Power

I floated with my feet two inches above the ground, a perfumed cloud of euphoria, carried like a pharaoh by a team of slaves. I had no will but Aletha's and Rogers's. I let the wind tell me which way to walk. The icy wind of January. I had no idea what I was doing, who I was, where I was.

Back in the hotel, the burner phone that I'd left there rang. The fat one, Thing One, with the deep voice bellowed, "Where the hell you been?"

"She abducted and tortured me. What can I say? I wasn't able to find out anything because I was gagged most of the time, couldn't even talk."

"Really?"

"You have to believe me."

"Well, no, we don't have to believe you. But if it's true we could have her arrested. Kidnapping. Federal offense."

"I don't think that would be a good idea."

"No, I wouldn't think you would like that, exposing your...idiosyncrasies..."

"One thing I learned. She has a collaborator named Roger."

"Roger what?"

"I never got a formal introduction. Handsome Black man. I'm meeting her again next week. I'll have something for you then."

Silence. Then: "Okay. But you need to call in every day."

I gnashed my teeth and listened to the messages on my iPhone. Several from Matthew, first just how ya doing, there's a meeting, turning ever more concerned for my whereabouts. "Have you been abducted by aliens?"

Following my nose, I found myself at the meeting about fighting Mass Incarceration. The group had grown – about 40 people – all kinds of people. I was pleased to see Matthew facilitating the meeting.

The first half was wisely devoted to introductions: "Your name and how you got here." People wouldn't stop. Stories of being railroaded into jail, police brutality, prison life. Being in the SHU, solitary confinement. One man had been in jail for seven years awaiting trial on a minor drug offense – of which he maintained he was innocent – until they finally dropped the charges.

The energy of the meeting was palpable, way different from that first meeting a couple months back. For one thing, most of the people were Black, people for whom the issue of criminalization was not abstract. "A Black man is killed by the police every 28 minutes," one of the participants reported,

The meeting broke into committees to plan for the

conference: Program, Outreach/Publicity, Logistics, Fundraising. I went to the Outreach committee and suggested that we try to contact some of the gang leaders in town. "Do you know how to do that?" the young woman facilitating asked me. She was dark skinned, heavy set, strong voiced.

"No, I'm kind of new in town."

That killed that discussion.

Before the meeting adjourned, Matthew summarized. He said, "You know, people, we can have this conference and we can have marches and demonstrations. But we just might have to think about taking over this city."

There was a pause, a pregnant pause. Followed by cheering.

After the meeting, I went with Matthew to Starbucks. "What did you mean by that 'taking over the city' business?"

"You know, I'm not really sure. It just seems like the next step, unless we're going to just roll over and accept defeat on all these cases. It was partly your influence, your insistence that a conference wasn't enough. I suppose it would be like Occupy, but with real people, not just wild-eyed activists."

"You mean Black people."

"I do. I mean Black people. No offense."

"None taken. You are still the majority in this town."

"Only barely. Gentrification has taken its toll. But there are some hopeful developments."

"Like what?"

"We're calling it the Progressive Alliance, after Richmond, California."

"Yeah, I know about them. Took the town away from Chevron for a while."

"There's the fringy green group called DC Statehood Green Party. They field losing candidates year after year, seem intent on staying small so they can stay pure. Then there's a bunch of Democratic Party clubs, Fredrick Douglass, Paul Wellstone. Some meetings are coming together. All around the pending Supreme Court decisions."

This all sounded exciting, but there was a limit to what I could do. Every four hours or so, I would receive a severe jolt in my crotch, just so Aletha could remind me of who was in control.

But somehow, I dragged myself to my 12-step program. I told the group how stuck I was on giving up control. Pondering the knotty Higher Power conundrum, my addled brain drifted into an excruciating headache. Why is some pain erotic, but some just not? I had to leave the meeting before the end, followed by looks of sympathetic condemnation.

When I got back to my hotel, I scarfed a bunch of painkillers, smoked some marijuana, newly legal in DC.

A lot of times when I smoke weed, I can get these profound visions that in the light of day are just silly. But this one stuck: What if we're looking in the wrong place for old Higher Power? What if "he" or "she" or "it" isn't big at all, but the smallest thing you could think of, like a hydrogen atom. Maybe a single hydrogen atom really started this whole universe off. So on some peculiar level of fiction I got in touch with this singularity, the first atom:

> *I was the first hydrogen atom, at least in this universe. There were just a few charges floating around in nothingness. My Dad was a plus and my Mom a minus. Or the other way around. There is a fundamental equality in the universe of us hydrogen atoms. So there I was, something new. I didn't know where I was, who I was, what I was doing there. (Kind of how I think you humans feel most days). I knew only that I was.*
>
> *There was something else though: there was an energy that came from my parents. In those days of precious little matter, a sense of incompleteness. A desire, as it were. A yearning.*
>
> *There was no time yet. Not even a yet. I created that later. So I don't know how long I waited. But I sensed it deep in my minimal gravity, that there was another one of us somewhere. There was no space or distance then or precious little. So I don't know how it happened, but at some point, there were two of us. We felt awkward at first – both of us I think. We were the same, after all. Identical. A couple of eons, or maybe it was just seconds before we even had the nerve to acknowledge each other's existence. But when our protons finally nodded, there was electricity between us. I suppose you could take that literally. For eons, or maybe seconds, we danced around each other, our*

negative rings simultaneously attracting and repelling us. We became inseparable. It made both of us realize how lonely we had been. There was something weird about it. Like falling in love with your image in the mirror. Narcissistic and incestuous at the same time.

The attraction became stronger, a sense in both of us that we wanted to merge. Wrap our rings around each other and bring our sputtering nuclei together. But there was also a sense that we would lose something in that intensity of a relationship. Our individuality. It made us giddy to think that if we merged ourselves, we would destroy hydrogen. There were only a few of us. Maybe only two. And we were, by some standards, small. So we didn't do anything. We waited. For eons, or maybe only seconds.

Until one day – oh yeah, nothing like days yet – one moment there were three of us. I was shocked at my reaction. Rather than delighted, welcoming this new entity into our growing universe, I was jealous. My partner, I'll call him Adam just to confuse you, was immediately attracted to this interloper. But after some kind of while, reason returned and I began to think of how this third party freed us. We didn't need to worry about ending the brief existence of hydrogen if Adam and I merged.

That however, wasn't in the stars, which didn't exist yet, either. Adam was drawn toward Three. I couldn't stop it, nor could I understand it. We were identical for plus sake. What did it see in Three that it didn't see in me? Well, see isn't quite right. Feel.

What did it feel in Three that it didn't feel in me? I know most humans don't think that creatures as small and "dead" as us hydrogen atoms could feel anything, but the basis of feelings is attraction and repulsion and we had that in spades. So yes, that imbalance between repulsion and attraction with repulsion stronger – we experience that as sorrow. Just like you do. So I gave them, Adam and Three, my blessing. I was concerned what would happen if these two truly married, merged their beings together. Maybe it would destroy the universe. Certainly we all three knew there was a shitload of energy involved. And so those two fused and ignited what you now call, appropriately, the Big Bang.

The cold winds still buffeted me about, but the cold was sinking into my bones. California dreaming. The cold in our hearts bonded Aletha and me – this ultimate kind of coldness that if you allowed yourself to fully feel it, you could get to the other side, into the warmth.

When I got the text from Aletha and Roger, my groin swelled, setting off a jolt. My body smiled in a way that was hard to argue with. I took a long shower, Naired my body hair, painted my toenails a slutty bright red. I splattered myself with Chanel #5, and, heart-beating, blood-pumping, put on the black Spandex bicycle racing outfit, walked the six blocks to arrive at Union Station by 7:00 AM. I waited forty agonizing minutes, understanding that my tormentors were enjoying every minute of my agony.

Finally the van pulled up. The door opened. No one needed to grab me. I sat primly in the back seat. Their greetings were kind, and knowing, fully aware of their power over me.

"Put the blindfold on," Aletha said. "We still don't want you to know exactly where we're taking you. Besides, you look cute in a blindfold." I strapped it onto my head.

"Remember *The Story of O*?"

"Of course," I said, my buttocks clenching.

"Do it! Pull your pants and your panties down and sit with your bare ass on the seat."

"Yes, Ma'am."

"Think about how that tingly ass of yours will feel once it's had the beating it craves."

"Yes, Ma'am."

"You seem really pleased to see us, Pamela. That's good. That's very good. Your training is going swimmingly." Her voice became hypnotic. "You must fully surrender to us, Pamela. We know you told us that you have surrendered. But such a surrender must be constantly tested and reinforced, because you cannot fail us in the mission we ultimately will be sending you on."

"What mission is that?" I asked impassively, reaching for surrender mode.

Silence. A hardening of tone. "You will be told when the time comes. Meanwhile, we all have a lot of work to do."

They took me back to the dungeon. As we walked from the van, they handled me, one on each side, with tenderness. Inside, Aletha gently removed my clothes and hugged me long and hard. She didn't remove the locked cage from my cock, but she turned off the tens unit so I wouldn't get shocked every time it hardened. They took me to another room, which was dark and gothic, but had a king size bed. They cuffed my hands and spread-eagled me on the bed, then they both rubbed me. They massaged me expertly as I lay on my back, with only occasional genital teases. They uncuffed me, flipped me over, recuffed me, and worked on my back, my thighs, my ass. They spent what felt like hours with my asshole, greasing it up, rubbing it with their hands, slowly edging their fingers inside. My body began to writhe.

"That's it, Pamela," Roger said in his deep voice. "Breathe into your female nature. You're a slut. You're a whore. And you love every minute of it."

Gentle as they were being, the massage ended and the spanking began. It was Roger, alternating between butt cheeks with that excruciatingly cruel rhythm he had – that hesitation between each blow that made me whimper in anticipation.

At the end of the short spanking, Aletha removed all her clothes and lay her body on top of mine, sprawled on my stomach. My cock squeezed against its cage, my balls no doubt blue, aching as if squeezed in a vice.

She strapped the ball gag into my mouth. Then she showed me the hypodermic needle. "Pamela, we are going to make you into a full-time sissy for real, no more role playing. It's good that you removed your disgusting male hair. Your toenails are lovely. Now we're going to transform the rest of you. These are female hormones. You will feel your body begin to feminize within a few days. You will enjoy it." The injection penetrated my left butt cheek.

Roger put something else in front of my face, a wooden handled six-inch metal spike ending with a flattened message: Gothic letters reading MA. Aletha Maxwell, backwards. "This is a branding iron, Pamela."

I squirmed in my restraints. I was not ready for this.

"I'm going to heat it here, where you can see it turning red and imagine how it will feel when I apply it to your ass." He set it up on a ring stand above a Bunsen burner, just like high school chemistry.

They waited in silence while I watched the branding iron turn orange, then red, then nearly white. They tightened the restraints on my ankles and wrists so I could barely move.

"I won't lie to you, Pamela," Roger said softly. "This is going to hurt. Your ancestors used to do this to my ancestors. A proper slave wears a brand."

They positioned themselves on chairs, one on each side, within reach of my ass. "One more thing," Aletha said. "You must consent. Do you consent to us branding you, Pamela, Peter Graves?" She unsnapped my gag so I could speak.

I was silent.

"Okay, Aletha," Roger said. "We'll need the inflatable hood we had so much fun with last time." Aletha rose to get it.

"It's okay," I said hastily. "I consent."

"You consent to what?" Aletha asked.

"Wearing your brand."

"Good girl." She replaced the gag. "You'll need this to bite on."

Roger applied alcohol to the meaty center of my right butt cheek.

With a rhythm similar to his spankings, Roger brought the iron to my butt so I could feel the warmth, then withdrew it, heated it some more, teased my butt with it again, and then slammed it onto my ass.

Despite the gag, I screamed my loudest scream. I'd never felt anything quite like this. The spasm of pain was immediately relieved by a rush of endorphins – I relaxed into the pain. I became one with the pain, Aletha and Roger each lying beside me, soothing me as I sobbed.

I slipped into my astral subspace. There seemed to be a truce declared as my being dealt with the excruciating pain of the brand. I saw the rodent again. My speck of consciousness tried to chase it again. I got a better look. It was a mouse. *The dormouse?*

Responsibly, they covered the brand with antibiotic ointment and a large Band-Aid. "You'll feel this for a while," Roger said unnecessarily.

They let me sleep for about six hours, though time was once more losing meaning.

When they turned me over and refastened the cuffs, they layered some medical adhesive on my chest. Over each of my nipples, they placed a very realistic silicone breast. They also glued some padding to round out my hips.

They invited me to stand before them in front of a tri-fold mirror. They lovingly dressed me in deep purple bra and panties that fit as though designed for my transforming body. Aletha wrapped me with a lacy corset in matching purple, and Roger laced it from the rear to hourglass my figure – or try.

They garnished me with a matching garter belt and white silk thigh-high stockings, then slipped over my shoulders a burgundy velvet mini dress with a lace collar. My favorite color. They stepped me into burgundy heels, medium high. Something I could manage as I learned. "Training wheels," Roger laughed.

They stepped back to admire their work. I was in la-la land again, deep subspace, reserved for a female sensibility, deeper than ever, way deeper. I obliged them by turning about like a fashion model, wiggling my hips.

"Very nice, Pamela." Roger said.

"Good. Good girl," Aletha confirmed.

They sat me at a dressing table with a mirror surrounded by Hollywood starlet lights. Aletha put a plastic bib on me and did my make-up. Foundation, mascara, red lipstick, eyebrow pencil. Gold ring clip-on earrings – I hadn't been pierced yet. And a wig – a salt-and-pepper wig, realistic like you rarely see.

Long, straight, in a ponytail down my back. How Joan Baez would have looked if she hadn't cut her hair.

Aletha brushed my hair and combed into it some magenta powder, tempera paint. "I'm 'youth-enizing' you Pamela. Be glad I'm not euthanizing you." She and Roger roared with laughter at her joke.

They stood me before the tri-fold mirror and admired their work.

"Pamela, you're beautiful," Roger said with a tremor in his confident voice that suggested the possibility of serious attraction to his creation.

"Say this," Aletha commanded. "My name is Pamela and I'll be your slut tonight."

I repeated in what I thought was my sexiest voice, "My name is Pamela, and I'll be your slut tonight."

Aletha and Roger looked at each other knowingly. Aletha said, "Maybe your voice will improve when the hormones kick in."

"Or we could go to plan B," Roger said.

"Plan B. Cut off those nasty testicles."

"No," I said involuntarily. I immediately regretted my lack of self-control.

"'No,' Pamela? You have the temerity to say 'no' to us, after all this time? Assume the position."

I fell to my knees, flipped up my dress and slipped my panties down.

"How's that brand of yours doing?" Roger said as he ripped off the Band-Aid. "Still looks a little raw. We better disinfect it." He dabbed it with alcohol. I felt burned all over again, only with white hot needles penetrating deep into my flesh. I screamed.

"That's good, Pamela," Aletha said. "Go ahead and scream. We like to hear you scream. Now we have a treat for you. Except for that one 'no,' you've been a good girl. How long since you've come, Pamela?"

"Since you put the cock cage on two weeks ago."

"That's a long time." She unlocked the padlock and removed the cage. My cock sighed with relief and promptly responded to Aletha stroking my balls. She could be so gentle. "Yes, I think it's ready. You will come only when I tell you to, Pamela. Pull up your panties, we don't want to soil your dress. Have you ever sucked cock before?"

"No," I said in a small voice.

"You're in for a treat, girl. Stay on your knees, but keep your dress up, because I'll need to train you to do it right." Roger, already shirtless, stepped out of his leather pants, and stood before me fully naked and fully erect. His lean body was hairless. He slithered toward me so his erection was an inch from my nose.

"Look at it, Pamela. It's beautiful, isn't it?" He did have a full ten inches, though it was relatively slender.

Aletha reached for her riding crop and whacked me on my brand. "You can touch his balls, Pamela. Have you ever touched another man's balls?"

"No," I whispered. My own cock was throbbing. I touched his balls. *Was I gay all this time?* I didn't want to, but I was liking this.

"Kiss it," Aletha said.

I kissed it on the head. And all up and down the shaft.

"That's right." She whacked me again on the other side. "Now put it in your mouth."

I went down as far as I could, about three inches. She whacked me again. "Open your throat, slut!"

I opened my throat. Roger stuck his cock all the way back, a full eight inches. Whack! "No gagging!" Aletha said.

I closed my eyes and wrapped my mouth around Roger's cock as lovingly as I could. I stroked his balls.

Out of the corner of my eye, I saw Aletha step up behind Roger, rubbing her front against his back. "Suck it, slut," she said. "Suck it, my little faggot."

I felt Roger begin to spasm. "Take his come, Pamela. Swallow it."

The spurt was salty and fishy, an oyster shot into my mouth from a paint ball gun.

"Now come, Pamela. Come in your panties."

It gushed out of me in waves and spurts. My body writhed and spasmed.

"Good girl, Pamela, good girl." Aletha gently stroked my ass, avoiding the brand which still throbbed.

11

The Conference

They sent me back out into the world a softer person, fleshy, luscious, in my panties and cock cage. I was in love with my captors – Stockholm all the way, Patty Hearst, Nicholas Brody in *Homeland*. I spent a week at the Manolo, lying on my belly to heal the brand. Propped on my elbows, I read.

Justice Johnson's memoir mentions the profound influence of Ayn Rand on his political philosophy. I knew she was a darling of the right. I knew nothing of her writing. I started with *The Fountainhead*, which I downloaded off Piratebay. I was surprised at the complexity of the emotional landscape. Dominique. Dominique, who orchestrated her own rape by the hero. Later the feminists went apeshit, but to me the rape fit within the moral universe of my own sexuality. True, I was increasingly sympathetic to sadomasochism as I experienced it, I also felt that the sub male/dominant female dynamic which contradicted traditional sex roles, was fundamentally different than the sub female/dominant male dynamic, that reinforced the oppressive pattern of sexism. Still, as Aletha said after our first foray, you like what you like.

Johnson managed to ignore Rand's atheism while embracing her individualism. One can see the self-serving narrative of the "successful" people: we are so selfish we do no harm. We deserve our privilege. We are the Creators. Lacking a Higher-Power-type God, we are gods. True Wagnerian heroes.

A cosmic headache took off where the last page ended. My consciousness was travelling. When I reached the astral plane where the epic battle between The Peter Defense Forces and the The Big C was raging, I again spotted the mouse scurrying toward me. I recognized him. "Frank," I greeted.

I was in some realm between life and death. When I was about eight years old, I found two baby mice in the basement. Fell deeply in love with them, naming them "Frank" and "Stein." They were tiny, half the size of their three-inch tails. I kept them in one of those plastic habitat things, but would occasionally bring them out to play on the day bed. Unfortunately, I also liked to use the bed as a trampoline. One afternoon, jumping joyfully, I smashed both the mice with my feet. Now one was here giving me advice.

Was it English? I don't know. In the midst of battle, Frank asked why was I planning to die for killing a Supreme Court Justice in order for the court to approve a cancer treatment that would keep me alive.

It made me think. Maybe a meaningful death wasn't as important as a meaningful life. Or maybe my addled brain had gone completely haywire.

The conference convened in mid-April. The smell of a Movement with a capital M was in the air, along with spring's cherry blossoms. Aletha and Roger were leaving me alone. Though I hadn't had an orgasm since sucking off Roger, I wasn't thinking about sex. I was thinking about building the Movement. There was much debate over our name. We finally came up with the National Alliance for Justice Conference, bringing together the constituencies that each of the four court cases represented. The conference convened at All Souls Unitarian Church. I played the role of a gopher, trying to help everybody out. The troubleshooter. I ejected a drunk from the premises. I managed to catch snatches of the workshops – know your rights, how to keep your children out of jail, labor organizing, abortion rights, reducing carbon emissions. I wanted to be in one of the more exciting workshops, but there was no one else to do the cancer workshop, so I had to lead it. "The Stem Cell Decision and Cancer."

About ten people came to the workshop, five of whom were astrocytoma survivors, the one cancer, now incurable, that might be cured if the proper stem cells were allowed to be developed. We had a hushed informal support group after the workshop. Many of us had the same question. A droopy man with hardly a foot out of the grave blurted it out: "Ever imagine going down to the cellular level?" I thought of all those strange visits to what I called the "astral plain" where I could witness the battle between the cancer cells and my inadequate immune system composed of T-cells, white blood cells, and a very few Stem Cells. Four of the five of us had similar experiences with this microscopic field of battle. It was an enormous relief to hear this, and we laughed.

At the final plenary session, I glimpsed that at least half the participants were refreshingly young. One demand emerged: vote NO on all four appeals. The leaders had, rightly or wrongly, squashed more militant demands like DC statehood, stopping enforcement of discriminatory drug laws, creating jobs. I wasn't sure how I felt. I liked the simplicity of the single demand, but I was sick of playing defense. I wanted the energy the movement was generating to go further – into offensive territory. But the people had voted. The confab was just about ending without having proposed a plan to win this demand.

Meanwhile, my headache came back with a vengeance. Despite some elation at the success of the conference, my eyeballs were pulsating. I was nauseous. I felt an attack of diarrhea coming on. I wanted nothing more than to curl up in a fetal position on my bed.

Still, I went to the microphone. "We can't just leave it like this. Feel the power in this room. Don't let it dissipate. Let's occupy the Supreme Court. Let's go home from here, grab a bite to eat along with our sleeping bags. I know it's been awhile since the Occupy movements, but we've learned some things since then. Let's meet in front of the Supreme Court at 6 PM." Thunderous applause. Passed by acclamation.

The occupation took place without a hitch. There wasn't a cop or Federal Marshall to be seen. Focusing on the people as they arrived, breathing into the excitement of the present moment, I passed beyond the lethal headache. About 200 people gathered on the oval plaza between the two fountains on the First Street side of the Supreme Court Building.

It was warm and still light when we started trickling in. The first chant to burst spontaneously from the crowd was a reading of the inscription above the portico: "Equal Justice Under Law."

The Occupy movement had been unable to sustain itself with its anarchistic rejection of leadership. While it made sense that anarchism would prevail as the ideology of the left after the collapse of the communist movement, it couldn't transcend its own contradictions. How do you lead a movement if you disparage the entire concept of leadership?

Matthew had turned me on to a Facebook group reading *Rebel Cities*, by David Harvey. His argument is that urbanization, rather than industrial production, is now the primary engine of capitalism. So revolutionaries should focus on organizing cities, using the Paris Commune as their model and inspiration.

Might we be able to steer this neo-Occupy movement instigated by the Supreme Court likely overstepping its authority toward organizing the city? This was an exciting possibility.

A possibility that eclipsed my need or desire to assassinate anyone.

I attached myself to Matthew, the one leader the white anarchists (there were hardly any Black ones) would be unlikely to attack. As we met up on the steps that evening, he said to me, "Now what?"

"Huh?" I said.

"You're the one who proposed this occupation. Do we just stay here forever?" There was a trace of spite in his voice.

"Until the court makes its decisions?"

"Okay. A month then. Can we keep people here for a month? Some of us have to work, some of us have families. Will they let us stay here a month?"

"Who knows? Probably not," I said.

There was a landing about halfway up the massive staircase in front of the Supreme Court building. The impromptu stage for this event. Roots Smiley, a light skinned rapper with a huge natural and sideburns to his chin, seized the day. He began rapping about revolution.

"Matthew, you were the one preaching about taking over the city, remember? Isn't this an opportunity to set up an alternative government, a rebel city?"

"Yeah, but we're not ready."

"We will never be ready," I said

"That's probably true."

"So, it's funny I've never asked, but do you have a family?"

"My wife Clarissa and four-year-old Imani. It's going to be tough to be here for a month. Maybe they'll come for a day or two. And you do know I have a job with Ceasefire."

"Oh, yeah, the ex-gang folks."

"Some not so ex."

"Maybe you could persuade some of them to come here, hang out with us."

"Really, Peter? I don't think you want that."

"I defer to your judgment, Matt."

"Meanwhile, this was your idea to come here. We need to organize this body to become the DC Commune." Matthew's voice dripped with sarcasm. "I mean, don't get me wrong, I'm all for it. But do forgive my skepticism."

"Okay, but you and me, okay? We step into the vacuum and do this thing?"

"All right, Peter. You go first."

After Roots had finished his rap, I stepped up to the stage. "Mic check," I said, a little tentatively, not really hip to the lingo of the Occupy rituals.

The crowd echoed, "Mic check."

"I'd like to help get us organized. We need some committees to deal with food, water, press…"

Someone interrupted. "You have to let us repeat what you say."

"Oh. Sorry, I forgot. I'll start again. "I'd like to help get us organized." The crowd echoed my words. "We need a food committee." Echo. "Food committee meet by the fountain on the left." I pointed. My words rippled across the plaza.

Committees brought food, water, sleeping bags. Portable toilets and tents were delivered. Songs were sung. Wine bottles and joints passed around.

Someone hooked up their iPhone to a Bose Bluetooth speaker and played Martha and the Vandellas' "Dancing in the Street." Dancing went on for an hour or so. Thanks to Twitter, the crowd grew. Close to 300 people slept on the steps.

I was in my element. The whole idea of assassinating anyone – even writing about it – seemed absurd. This is what we needed – a serious movement. I was flitting around the plaza like a mad general trying to lead it, or, to be fair to myself, offering my experience. I had nothing to lose. That gave me power.

Matthew suggested calling a meeting of all the groups coalescing around the four Supreme Court decisions. Noon the next day at the Capitol Hill Baptist Church, three blocks from where we were.

At about 5 o'clock that evening a huge jolt in my groin and a buzz on my phone notified me of the arrival of instructions. "The time is now. Go to the corner of 3rd and Constitution at 6 PM."

I gathered my strength. "No," I texted back. "It's all unfolding perfectly."

My knees buckled and I fell on the ground from the next jolt. Comrades surrounded me with concern. "What's wrong?" they asked.

"Nothing." I was deeply embarrassed. I stood up and went about my business. Stronger jolt. I fell down and screamed. Before it happened again or somebody called an ambulance, I texted back "K."

12

The Penultimate Submission

At five to six, I ran the two blocks. The van approached. I climbed inside. Roger was driving, Aletha riding shotgun. She looked at me. I knew what she wanted. She wanted me to do that "O" thing of lowering my pants and my panties and having my naked butt against the Naugahyde upholstery. But I wasn't having it. I was feeling powerful. I could resist Roger and Aletha. At the same time, I did feel my cock filling its cage, dangerously close to completing the circuit for another jolt. But it was learning how to control its tumescence. Precisely.

Aletha looked at me in a penetrating way as if deliciously challenged by my resistance. I could see her devious mind working beneath her wild corkscrew hair. Devising all kinds of painful humiliations to bring me back in line. The erotic power in our dynamic was more intense than ever. She sighed. I translated: *okay, for now, we'll see.* She knew better than to challenge my resistance too harshly, to allow the erotic power in the air to build.

"You've become quite the leader, Pamela," Aletha said conversationally. She was wearing that knee length leather shirt-dress with all the buttons.

How does she know? Oh. Former CIA.

"Mmm," I said non-committally.

She hooded my head so I wouldn't see where we were going, though I knew it would be back to the dungeon place.

"It seems like you've been, how shall we say, straying from the program, Pamela."

Even though I knew it would cost me later any number of lashes and torments, I remained stubbornly silent.

"Now I remember. You are a..." She paused. "...glutton for punishment."

Her mind was working with laser-like efficiency, her pauses calculated. Saliva filled my mouth like pre-cum.

"If I were you right now, I would hold my berries fondly. Tell them good-bye."

Pause.

"You will submit, Pamela. One way or another."

She's bluffing. She wouldn't do that.

"Good thing we stocked up on butter and garlic, huh, Rog?"

He emitted an evil chuckle. "I feel like a starving lion smelling fresh meat."

Roger said, "Tonight's your night, Pamela."

I had no idea what he meant, but the idea stiffened me up enough for a short jolt.

"Careful, Pammy," Aletha said. "Control yourself."

Back in the dungeon, without further talk, they stripped off my clothes and chained my wrists and ankles face up on a table. Aletha strapped on a ball gag. Roger brought up a large roll of industrial strength Saran wrap. They began wrapping me from my feet till I couldn't breathe. It took only seconds to panic. I could vaguely see through the transparent film – Aletha was talking to me, but all I could hear was an incoherent mumbling. I assumed they were asking for my surrender. I screamed "Yes! I surrender!" as loud as I could, afraid they couldn't hear me. As I felt myself drifting toward blacking out, I heard a rip in the fabric, and air rushed into my lungs.

A stab to one ear created an opening for hearing.

Another to my groin cut a hole so my cock and scrotum were exposed. Unbelievable – I could feel them removing the chastity cage. My cock was free!

"I'm sorry," Aletha said. "We need your absolute loyalty for our mission. We're going to remove your pesky testicles, Pamela." My fury translated to a noisy vibration of the plastic wrap. *What mission?*

"We want you to watch," Aletha said. The knife cut the cellophane in front of my eyes, exposing the industrial ceiling's ducts and tubes. Roger lifted the back of my head. Aletha waved some kind of large pliers, brought it close to my eyes. Like vise-grips but with prongs to stretch a rubber ring. "Pamela, this is called an elastrator. It will cut off circulation to your scrotum. In 12 hours, your balls will fall clean off. Not a drop of blood to worry about. See how humane we are? Roger, read me the instructions."

Roger's voice was excited. "*1*. Restrain the animal."

"Check," said Aletha. She began to gently stroke my scrotum. She even kissed it. "I'm kissing them good-bye for you, Pamela. Roger, do you think we should let him come one last time?"

"Hmmm." Roger smiled, looking me over. "Naw."

"**2.** Place a rubber ring on the prongs of the elastrator. Turn the elastrator so that the prongs face the kid's body. Expand the ring by squeezing the elastrator and place over the scrotum and testes. Position it as close to the kid's body as possible."

She kept stroking until I was on the verge. Then she slapped my penis with a wooden spoon. It shriveled. I felt the cold metal against my scrotum.

Roger continued: "**3.** Manipulate the scrotum until you are certain that both testes are descended below the ring."

"Yeah," Aletha said. "Let me manipulate that scrotum." She stroked it some more until my cock stood up again.

"**4.** Press the trigger lever, displacing the ring from the prongs, thereby positioning the ring. Note: Be sure that both testes are below the ring! If they are not, cut the ring and start over."

The band snapped onto my scrotum, like the biggest ever of Aletha's kick to my balls. I sucked in my breath and let out a small scream.

"You might as well scream, honey. Scream good-bye to your manhood, girl," Aletha said in her stage whisper.

"**5.** Administer an injection of tetanus antitoxin. Even though this is a bloodless procedure, the tetanus organism can gain entry through the irritated tissue around the rubber ring."

There was a sharp stab to the side of my left butt cheek. Aletha said, "Here's your tetanus, Pamela. A nice cocktail, so to speak, with some more of your female hormones. We're done now. Good night, Pamela." She kissed me on the ball gag. "When you've healed from this procedure, we'll continue your transformation."

Roger said, "Maybe we should tell him now that he's so...receptive."

"Hmmm," Aletha grunted. "Okay. Pamela, we are making your dream come true. It just so happens that your friend Sylvester Johnson likes sissy boys. Don't ask me how I know this. Oh, well, ask me if you want. Oh, you can't talk. We are training you to – briefly – become his lover and then his assassin."

You said you didn't know him! But of course I couldn't speak.

"That son of a bitch got me fired from the CIA," she continued. "You might as well know the whole story. I was his procurer, his pimp. I would round up sissy boys for him to take out on his yacht where his protectors could only follow in little motorboats. He owed me for that. He paid me like a hundred bucks per hook up. Christ. He owed me, Pamela. Do you hear me? All I asked for was $2500 a month to keep quiet. He went to the CIA and the next thing I know is I'm fucking fired.

"I tried to go to the press with everything I knew about Johnson, but the CIA beat me to it by having me portrayed as some kind of delusional lunatic who wasn't to be believed. Then you came along with your cockamamie story which fit so perfectly with mine. So here we are."

I started to cry. Not just for being trapped in the Saran wrap. Not just for full claustrophobic panic. And not just at being trapped into committing murder after all. But most of all for my balls. Never again would I be able to enjoy that spasm of ecstatic release that makes life worth living. Never again would my body shudder as every single neuron screamed with joy.

I cried until the plastic sack I was in filled with water from my tears. The room fell silent and then dark, darker than the darkest black hole in space. They were going to leave me like this. I cried and writhed and panicked and screamed and pressed against the restraints with all my might, until I tired myself out and fell into the death-like sleep of utter despair. I drifted in and out of sleep for what must have been days.

Hunger finally woke me all the way up. It was still as dark as deep space. Buried in the densest fog of despair, my sex life – my life – definitely over. I supposed it was just as well that soon I would be sent on this suicide mission.

My peephole of consciousness drifted down to the cellular level, the astral plane. On the field of battle, the spikey soccer balls of astrocytoma, the cancer cells, were advancing rapidly against the PDF. Frank the mouse shape-shifted toward my ear and messaged me. "Your despair is weakening those of us trying to keep you alive. Don't worry. It's going to be okay."

"Really? What's okay about losing my fucking balls?"

Then I noticed something else. I had a throbbing hard-on. Really? With no balls?

After a while, Aletha and Roger came for me, both naked and fuzzy with each other, as if they had just finished making love. I felt jealous, perhaps because I would never get to bask in that afterglow again myself.

Roger stuck the scissors in at the top of my head and cut through the Saran Wrap down to my feet. Aletha put her hand on my still erect scrotumless penis and smiled, pleased with her handiwork. But there was something else in that smile. I couldn't dare believe it. I pulled against the cuffs on my wrist. She unfastened them and continued to smile as she watched me touch myself. I still had one testicle! They'd left me one testicle! I can't think of a time when I have ever been more grateful for such a generous gesture. I still had one ball!

I knew there was something metaphorical here about the human condition at present: Thank you, thank you, thank you for not killing me. We have set a very low bar for how our rulers, our masters, treat us.

"You see how kind we are, Pamela," Aletha said sweetly. "You are one lucky girl. And you are in for yet another treat." They unfastened the shackles and took me, one on each arm, into the shower, where they lovingly washed me and shaved me all over of the stubble which had emerged since my last Nairing. They spent extra time on the cute little nubbins of breasts that were emerging thanks to the hormone treatments. `

Silently they dried me, had me kneel in the tub and administered an enema. They watched me lovingly while my bowels sputtered and drained.

They attached the silicone breasts and hip pads and dressed me in a matching set of robin's egg blue, lace-trimmed boycut panties, bra, waist-slimming corset and silky camisole. They slipped thigh high stockings on my legs and sparkly blue high heels on my feet. They fit my head with my gray Joan Baez ponytail wig with the magenta tempera highlights and sprayed me with Channel #5. With every gesture, they rubbed their naked bodies against mine, causing my poor single ball to swell and my cock to verge on exploding. "Not yet, honey," Aletha said.

I was placed in front of the mirrored vanity, hands cuffed behind me while Aletha did my make-up. They fed me raw oysters and kumquats. I was famished, hadn't eaten in who knows how many days. They released my hands.

"We have another oyster for you, Pamela. Come with me." I followed her into a tiny kitchenette area which I hadn't noticed before. On the stove was a small frying pan with melted butter and garlic. "I've done some of the prep for you."

Then she pulled a small plate from the tiny fridge. In the center was what looked like a purple bird egg. She smiled at me. My left testicle. "I've cleaned it for you. Now you will engage is the ultimate submission. You will sauté this mountain oyster and eat it."

Tears started down my cheek. "Don't cry, Pamela. You'll ruin your make-up," she warned. I drifted down into subspace. I plopped the ball in the butter. Like a phantom limb, I could feel it cooking. I rolled it around in the pan for a good ten minutes then set it back on the plate.

They sat me down at the vanity again. "Go ahead, Pamela." I picked up the testicle delicately as if sipping from a teacup and popped it in my mouth. I started crying again. But I was so grateful that they had saved my other one that I bit down and chewed. It tasted like sweetbreads, like a scallop, only chewy, more like a chunk of overcooked beef heart.

I had reached the depth of submission, as I was forced – was I really forced? – to cannibalize my own manhood. I felt utterly, deliciously, lost. They didn't rush me. "Go ahead, feel it, Pamela." Make-up or no, the tears flowed and time passed.

"Stand up, Pamela, and breathe into your glorious womanhood." Aletha's voice was dropping into a hypnotic mode. "Breathe into your feminine nature. Allow the *yin* energy to flow through your limbs." Her voice was soft and soothing. "Let the *shakti* spirit flow from your second *chakra* and percolate through your body. Soften, Pamela. Dance for us. Dance your seductive dance. Dance for Roger, Pamela. Submit to him. Turn him on."

I sank deeper into subspace. Roger clicked Norah Jones on his iPhone. I let whatever spirit had been unleashed move my body. I closed my eyes and slithered about the room, not knowing – not much caring – what might happen next.

What did happen was that Roger, naked Roger, embraced me and held me close, so close every part of my full frontal was touching him, his supple muscles. We danced a slow dance, hardly moving our feet at all, just rocking together to the music. I felt his erection in my belly just a little above mine.

He lifted my chin and kissed me full on the lips. We twisted our tongues together, we nibbled, we sucked each other's tongues. I was floating.

I slid down to my knees. I licked the shaft of his cock. I licked his balls. I could feel him begin to shiver. He pulled away gently. "I will come inside you, Pamela."

Years of homophobic conditioning had prevented me from indulging any fantasies I might have had of being fucked by a man. Yet here I was. Not feeling gay, exactly. Just girly.

He guided me over to a leather sling chair hanging on four chains. He pulled my panties all the way off. With Aletha's help, he buckled my arms to the straps above my head and my ankles in the air. While Aletha stood with her wiry-haired pussy next to my nose and stroked my head, Roger rubbed my cock, my ball, and my anus with liberal amounts of lube. Slowly. Ever so slowly. "You're tight, Pamela. I need you to open to me. Aletha?"

Aletha retrieved a rattan cane from the wall. She gave me ten mighty whacks. "Try it now," she said to Roger.

Roger lubed two of his fingers and slipped them easily inside me.

He lubed his own cock and I sucked in my breath in anticipation of what was to come.

He slid his cock into my virgin ass.

Oh. My. God. Oh. My. God.

He held it inside me without moving.

He slipped it slowly in and out three times. I screamed with girly pleasure. My cock erupted with a massive loogie of cum, spurting all the way to my face.

Roger grunted deep in his viscera. He shook, he quivered, he spasmed. He shouted. I felt his come deep inside me. My entire body smiled.

I would do anything for them.

13

Crossed Wires

Kissing both of them good-bye, I swished out of the van and into the Manolo, dressed in androgynous spandex, wiggling my hips with my new-found femininity, digging it – but, no wig, back to presenting as male. Smiling.

I remembered the pimply faced desk clerk – Seymour, his name was. I smiled at him.

He frowned back at me. "We figured you skipped town. We cleared out your room, dumped your stuff in the trash. You still owe us $120 dollars."

"My computer?"

He hesitated. "Dumped it."

"Really? You mean you sold it."

"You owed us money, man."

My novel. My novels. All that deathless prose. Now dead. My bubble of bliss, now pricked.

"Look, I couldn't help it. I was abducted for Christ's sake!"

"Oh, yeah, by aliens. We get a lot of that around here."

I seriously stretched my brain to think of some way to explain my situation to this fellow. But whatever I said, it wouldn't make sense. And mostly it wouldn't bring back my computer. "Well, can I have my room back, at least?"

"Soon as you pay up the back rent."

"You just said you sold my computer to pay the back rent."

He just looked at me. As if we were speaking different languages. I sighed. I took out my wallet and paid him $160. Without comment, he gave me the key to my old room.

I immediately regretted the payment. If I no longer had any of my belongings and my people were still sleeping out by the Supreme Court, why pay for this shithole?

I guess there was something about having a bed to sleep on if things got too crazy. I took a quick look at the room and hopped on the bus to 2nd Ave.

It both did and didn't surprise me that there was no one on the plaza in front of the Supreme Court except for some forlorn tourists disappointed that the court was not in session.

Where the hell was Matthew? I called him on my iPhone. No answer. There were no messages from him either.

I scrolled through the *Washington Post* headlines on my phone. I had been out of it for close to a week.

Three days ago, there'd been a sweep of the plaza at four in the morning. There had only been about 20 people there, and most went peacefully, enduring yet another defeat. There had been only one arrest: Matthew Taylor.

It was Monday night by now, and not much I could do. I called the police department, but they had no record in their jail of a Matthew Taylor. In the morning, I would find him. I would also shop for clothes and other essentials that had been tossed out. At least I still had some money left. It didn't appear that I would need any of it to hire an assassin. It seemed like I had drawn the straw myself. At minimal cost. Well, *practically* free.

Whether it was conditioning, brainwashing, or simply succumbing to torture, I didn't feel uncomfortable in my new role. I liked the Mata Hari aspect of it. I also liked that, true or not, I felt I had absolutely no choice in the matter. And, no small thing, I just might get my meaningful death.

Aletha and Roger had preserved my manhood and taken me to levels of ecstasy I could never have imagined. I had no one else. Not Mariana, not my daughters. Not even Matthew. I was on my own. I returned to my lonely room and curled up in bed, still breathing into my femininity. It was helpful to feel I had no control over the situation – like many women must feel much of the time. Surrender was my only option.

There was a knock. I can't say it was unexpected – I hadn't contacted my whatever-agency handlers for over a week, despite instructions to call them daily. And here they were, Thing One and Thing Two, Nosepicker and Ballscratcher. "You're coming with us," they stated matter-of-factly. I just smiled and went along. They took me to that same interrogation center where they took me before. This time they didn't bother to blindfold or hood me.

A blond, white woman with twinkly eyes and a friendly manner greeted me. She had that look of someone who may have dominated her share of men.

"Hi, Peter, Stacey Mulligan." Irish, I thought. "I'm CIA. I want to ask you some questions about your intentions to kill Supreme Court Justice Sylvester Johnson."

"You misunderstood," I gulped, not wanting to assume that they had heard the doctored tape.

"What's to misunderstand? You've been recorded on tape stating that you intended to kill Sylvester Johnson," she said calmly.

"I've been writing a novel. You know, a John Grisham, *Pelican Brief* sort of Washington thriller about a guy who tries to hire an assassin to kill a fictitious Supreme Court Judge."

"I've heard the tape. You said nothing about a novel."

"The tape's been doctored."

"Oh really? And who would do that and why? You have a copy of the novel?"

I sighed. The novel was on my confiscated computer. I really didn't want to rat out Aletha and Roger. They were all I had. For better or worse, they were what passed for my family.

She spread out pictures of me in panties spread-eagled on the bed. "We don't really care about your... peccadilloes. Though there are perhaps some people who would. Other than your family, I mean. We know your family has already seen them and pretty much written you off as a disgusting pervert. Which I guess you are, though I'm not here to judge you. There are some people in the movement who might think somewhat less of you if they saw these. People like..." She paused. "Matthew Taylor."

I unwisely winced at the mention of his name. "Where is he?"

"So you do know him."

"I know him."

"He certainly knows you. He's been telling us all about the little plot you two cooked up to assassinate Sylvester Johnson."

"Really?" I felt a sharp pain in my abdomen as if run through with a large butcher knife.

"Yes, sir. He said it was your idea, is that true?"

"I...I think I need a lawyer."

"Nonsense, you're not being charged with anything. You have the right to remain silent. Of course you do. This is America. You have free speech, too. Except when it comes to making homicidal threats against public officials. But charging you would cause problems for the Justice, which we don't want to do. We have free speech, too. We have the right to take these photographs to Matthew Taylor and show him what a little sissy faggot pervert he's been dealing with."

Her characterization stung, I wanted to cry, but I stared back, stone-faced. I'd seen enough *Homeland* and *The Wire* to be familiar with the tactic of telling each of us – Matthew and I – that we were ratting out the other. I seriously doubted it was true that he had ratted me out.

"So here's the deal," Stacey said. "We're about to release Taylor from jail. We want you to wear a wire and hang out with him. We need to know what your little movement is planning so it doesn't get out of hand. We don't want to see anyone hurt."

"Really?" I said. But I didn't want to have to explain the pictures to Matthew. He might be cool with it, he might not. I can't remember which episode of which show where the guy wearing the wire writes a note to the target telling him about the wire. I could do that.

"Can you just monitor everyone's cell phone? Wouldn't that be easier?"

"We used to be able to do that, but now you guys have gotten all sophisticated and use those new pirate servers that scramble signals so tracing is no longer possible."

"Okay," I said.

"Wow. That was a little too easy. Either you have less integrity than we thought, or you are planning to try to deceive us. The latter would be a big mistake."

"Don't worry. I won't try to deceive you," I lied.

"Okay. Taylor is being released tomorrow. Give him a day or so to spend with his family, then call him on Thursday. Meet up with him. Give your handlers a call on your burner a few minutes before you meet up."

"Okay."

She looked at me with deep skepticism, but, after showing me how to tape the tiny listening device to my chest, she let me go.

Back in my lonely, barren room, I couldn't stop thinking about Mariana, Lupe, and Marisol. Maybe family is all there is. If that sad thought was true, then I had nothing. Happy memories flooded my consciousness. Legoland, when the girls were five and seven, so proud as they earned their "drivers' licenses," scooting their little Lego cars around the track. Driving into Mexico, the first time for them, seeing their little eyes light up at the carnival teeming of Tijuana, the distinctive differentness from the U. S., at hearing everywhere their mother's language, which she'd been teaching them from day one.

The childhood near-disasters that brought us together. Like when we took three-year-old Lupe's temperature by mouth and she bit so hard the thermometer broke, filling her mouth with glass and toxic mercury. We rushed her to emergency, only to find that there was no glass and that the pure form of mercury in such thermometers wasn't toxic, only the oxides.

Once when we were camping, Lupe and the other ran away at the first sight of bees in the trees, leaving behind little Marisol, stung all over her body. We ran to find the ranger to make sure she wasn't allergic. He assured us if she was, she'd be dead by now. We plastered her with moistened baking soda.

The little game we made up, Marisol and I, "pic-tac-toe." Instead of X's and O's, we drew little pictures in the boxes, usually around some theme like animals or vehicles.

My heart constricted with what I had lost.

On Thursday I called Matthew, as instructed. "What do you want, Peter? I just got out. What the fuck happened to you? Your idea to occupy the Supreme Court. Then you just split."

"I'm sorry, Matthew. I told you I have this brain cancer, right? Sometimes I get these debilitating headaches that last for days. You saw me crumpled in a heap at the demo. It was all I could do to get back to my hotel and shut down for a couple of days."

Silence. "Okay. But you left us – me – hanging."

"Want to go for breakfast?" It was 11 o'clock in the morning.

"Okay. Denny's?"

"Denny's it is."

I hooked up the wire and brought my little legal pad. I called my handlers on the burner.

He was waiting for me in a booth when I got there. Striped oxford-cloth shirt with a button-down collar.

I ordered the Southwestern Skillet and passed Matthew a note. *I'm wearing a wire.*

He smiled. He wrote me a note. *That's funny. I am too.*

I had to repress a burst of laughter. I didn't want to explain any outbursts on tape. What is this, Spy vs. Spy from *Mad Magazine*? I wrote back, *They're either really incompetent or some kind of brilliant.*

The former, I think, hopelessly incompetent. How'd they get to you?

Came to my hotel.

I spoke up for the mike. "So, how was jail, Matthew?"

"Not that bad, really. They didn't torture me or anything. They asked about you, but I didn't tell them anything."

"Likewise. They tried to tell me you ratted me out, but I didn't believe them. So what's the next step in the movement?" I winked at him.

He wrote on the back of a leaflet, *Maybe we can use this situation.* I smiled.

He said out loud: "We're thinking about a die-in in the Capitol Building. About a week from now. We'll enter the building disguised as tourists, and then on a signal, suddenly lie down."

I tried to wrap my mind around what I knew must be disinformation. "Why the Capitol? Why not the Supreme Court?"

"They'll be expecting us to do something at the Supreme Court. It will be heavily guarded."

"I see. How's things at home, Matthew? How's your wife taking all this?"

"Not well. She's pissed that I spent so many nights at the occupation. She's pissed that I got arrested and we had to put up the house to post bond."

I wasn't sure whether this was real or disinformation. "I'm sorry. I know how it feels to be estranged from your family."

We exchanged sympathetic glances and mutually decided our work was done here. We gave each other a man-hug: shaking hands, pulling together, fists to backs.

14

The Mock Supreme Court

The court had postponed its decision on the four big cases to the very last day of its session, June 30. A week before it was expected to rule, our phones were all a-twitter about the die-in. Set to start as soon as the Capitol opened for tourists, 9 o'clock. But by 6 o'clock, a small contingent, notified by word of mouth, began trickling toward the Supreme Court Building.

The night before I had run into a woman dressed in full chador in front of my hotel. It was the grey haired white lady named Joyce who chaired the first coalition meeting I attended, in disguise. She whispered that Matthew's "estranged" wife Clarissa had hidden in the women's john in the Supreme Court Building and at 6 o'clock, would open a side entrance.

I couldn't believe that security wouldn't detect a breach like this, or that the building wouldn't be better guarded. But fortunately or unfortunately, competence was not the salient characteristic of the United States government.

People – mostly the trusted leaders who'd been active since the beginning – slipped into the building, about forty of us in all. We planned to occupy the courtroom itself, but the double doors were locked. Matthew, however, slipped a credit card between the doors. We looked at each other and grinned as the doors popped open. He assumed the chair of the Chief Justice. I of course assumed the chair of Sylvester Johnson.

By 9 o'clock, when the building officially opened, the chamber was filled with a couple hundred of our own people who had continued to trickle in by the side door.

Seated next to me was Clarissa, the woman of the hour. "You're my hero," I told her.

"T'weren't nothin," she drawled with false modesty. Her hair was a mass of braids, swirled around the top. She had a round face like the moon, light skin and freckles. Her body held extra weight with great dignity.

"Matthew told me you were upset with him for getting arrested and all. I take it that isn't true."

"Hardly. I can see where these Supreme Court decisions are headed. I don't want my daughter to grow up in an increasingly hostile society."

"Where's she now?"

"You didn't see Imani? She's sitting on Matthew's lap."

Indeed, a little girl with braids spiking out of her head like a Black Lisa Simpson waved to me.

"Weren't you scared to bring her here?"

"Very." She sucked in her breath and closed her eyes. "Very. But she insisted on coming. We've raised her like good small-D democrats. Democracy needs to start at age two. Children need to be given say over their own lives."

"That's pretty radical."

"It is, isn't it?" She smiled. "I hope it's not child abuse. I mean what if she sees her father get beaten by the police? What if *she* gets beaten by the police? I don't think it's come to that, not yet, but it could go that way in a heartbeat. It was that way not so long ago."

I looked us over as a group, the People's Supreme Court. "All we need now is the black robes."

As if on cue, a heavyset white woman with a doughy face approached the bench with an armload of black robes. "I found these in the laundry room." She handed them to the Justices.

The one she gave me smelled rancid. I guess they didn't change them all that often.

Matthew pounded his gavel, his size 11 shoe. "The People's Supreme Court is now in session."

His words echoing off the marble walls set off a mock trial – more like a mockery of a trial. Matthew told me they couldn't contact the press for this show, but they had a strong social media committee broadcasting the whole event on Facebook and Twitter.

A long-haired, bespectacled white man approached the bench and shouted out the name of a case. "Williams v. Florida."

Matthew declared: "The court sides with the Florida Supreme Court in throwing out the law rescinding the right to vote to people with more than one misdemeanor." The crowd cheered.

"Doe v. Virginia," an older Black woman called. "The abortion case."

Scratching his head as if to think of what to say next, Matthew declared, "The court rules that Roe v. Wade shall stand and that Doe should be allowed to have an abortion if she so chooses." The crowd cheered again.

A Black teenage boy approached the bench and called "Richmond v. Chevron."

Matthew looked around at the other judges, giving them a chance to join the charade. A Latina in her 20s with a baby in her arms declared, "The court finds for Richmond. The EPA and the City of Richmond have every right to restrict carbon emissions at the Chevron refinery."

Still more cheering.

I took up the next one: "Coalition of Cancer Cooperatives v. the United States. The court finds for cancer victims and throws out the law restricting the creation of new embryos and stem cells."

Victorious in all four cases. As the clamor died down, a man in a suit and tie with hair like wax shouted, "Citizens United." The crowd laughed – this one had cleared the court some years back.

Clarissa spoke up: "What the hell. As long as we have the power, let's throw that out and declare it unconstitutional for corporations to fund candidates. Corporations are NOT people!"

Applause.

Giddy, I turned to Clarissa. "This feels so weird. How long will they let us occupy this space?"

"Not long," she said. "I hope you're prepared to be arrested."

"No. I swore I'd die before going to jail again."

"Me neither. I have a plan…"

She was interrupted by someone shouting from the doorway: "The police are outside! There's hundreds of them."

It was only minutes before they strode in, clad in full riot gear. They started arresting people at the back.

"Can they do that?" I asked Clarissa. "There was no order to disperse."

"We're not just assembling. We're trespassing. They don't need an order."

"Are you a lawyer?" I asked jokingly.

"Matter of fact I am. Clerked for Justice Melissa Greenberg some years ago. I know this building."

"Oh!"

"Follow me. And tell the rest of the justices to follow."

"This court is adjourned," Matthew shouted.

Clarissa slipped out the back door before the cops reached us. We twisted down a narrow hallway past the laundry room, through another unmarked door that opened onto a narrow staircase.

"Not too many people know about these back stairs," Clarissa called over her shoulder. They're a cold war artifact that led to a serious fall-out shelter. Now they lead to a tunnel that goes to the parking garage. We used to call it the rabbit hole." She posted herself at the top and had people squeeze past her. "I'll stay here and watch for the cops."

The stairs went down three floors. The "justices" and a few of the people in the front rows could escape before Clarissa got a warning about the cops reaching the back. She sealed off the door.

The tunnel was totally dark. Around thirty of us, mostly the same ones who had led the occupation, jostled and bumped and cursed and apologized and giggled. My claustrophobia was squeezing sweat through my pores. We stopped at the door at the end of the tunnel. Clarissa twisted around people so that she could get to the front where Matthew, Imani, and I were squished. "I got people sitting in front of the door up top concealing it from the cops," she said.

She opened the lower door a crack, peered out. "Shit," she said. "The garage is crawling with cops."

"This surprises you?" I was unable to contain my annoyance.

"Actually, yes. I thought they wouldn't know about this tunnel. Maybe they still don't. Maybe they're just using the garage as a staging area. If we wait, maybe they'll go away."

"Maybe," I said.

Clarissa shouted a whisper that echoed down the line: "We just need to wait."

"I told you we shouldn't have brought her, Clarissa," Matthew scowled.

She glared at him. "You brought her, Matthew. You may recall that I spent the night in this august edifice, scared out of my wits that I would get caught. Why didn't we get a white guy to do this? Why did I volunteer? Because I knew I would get it right. I almost did."

I did not want to be in the middle of this. I wanted to dig a tunnel to escape these movement icons and their domestic squabble. The tunnel was hot and dark. Collective farts were growing dense. My heart was palpitating like a trapped coal miner. At least I knew we would survive. *Breathe. So we get arrested, so what? Breathe.*

"It was still your idea that she come," Matthew said sheepishly.

Imani began to cry.

I took her out of Matthew's arms. She screamed harder.

"It's okay, Imani. I'm Peter. I'm your Daddy's friend. It's going to be okay. I know it's scary. But everything will be all right. We'll play a game. You know this one? 'I spy with my little eye...'"

She squinted at me like I was crazy. "Everybody knows that game. But how we going to play down here? It's too dark. I spy something black."

"Everything," I said.

"Yup!"

I took out my iPhone to turn on the flashlight in order to play a game with Imani and saw that there were several texts from Aletha. "Union Station. 15 minutes." "Now." "Where are you?" 8:30, 8:45, 9:00. It was now 9:40.

Imani started crying again. "Just a minute, Imani. I need to answer this text."

Can't now. Check the news. There was no reception in this tunnel.

But I felt the sharp jolt to my genitals! Aletha must have some kind of super-connection.

My grunt broke the silence.

The jolts came now at increasingly shorter intervals. I jumped each time. Thirty seconds. Fifteen seconds. It didn't take a mathematician to tell where this was going. You'll never reach the end. Zeno's paradox. But so close to zero that it was like a constant pulse.

I doubled over screaming, both hands on my genitals. Clarissa and Matthew pushed me down on my back and started removing my pants to see what was wrong. "You have to stop screaming, Peter."

When they had my belt undone and my Levi's unbuttoned, it was they who grunted. I could only guess their reaction to the fuchsia panties. The wired cock cage. My guess is that they looked at each other knowingly – *I thought there was something strange about him.* I guessed a waft of disgust, a puff of pity, a gust of puzzlement. But movement veterans, they knew they had to put the interests of The People ahead of their feelings. They sent me out to the wolves. "Peter needs medical attention, so he's volunteered to see what the cops are up to."

By throwing me out the door they risked calling attention to themselves. In fact, it was downright weird that the cops hadn't discovered us yet. But

Matthew pushed the escape bar and opened the door just enough to dump my still cowering body on the concrete garage floor.

I lay there, fetal. Still as death. Fortunately, Aletha had stopped shocking me, in her kindly way. I waited a few minutes for a swarm of cops to encircle me. I was thinking how lucky I was to be white – I was sure they wouldn't beat me or kill me if I was perfectly still, not resisting

But there was no swarm. In the stillness, I crawled slowly along the wall, grateful for the refreshing carbon monoxide of the garage. I got ten feet from exit before I heard, "Hey!" and the patter of boots. Five cops surrounded me. Quiet, like they were looking at a corpse.

"Sir! Stand up!" came the gruff command.

I slowly pushed and pulled my crumpled body to my feet as if smoothing out a tube of paper, one of those Chinese lanterns we used to make.

Without a word, a cop on each side grabbed an arm and twisted it behind my back, attaching the Flex-i-cuffs.

I was still in death mode, a piece of flotsam on the surf of time. The electric shocks had sent me into subspace, but a new kind, superlatively unpleasant.

They stuffed me into the back of the black Ford SUV. The white cop behind the steering wheel had balding white hair, ruddy cheeks, and a toothbrush mustache. The cop riding shotgun was a Black man, a wisp of a person in a uniform three sizes too big.

The white guy asked politely, "What's your name, sir?"

I'd seen it on YouTube. "I don't answer questions."

"Really? You know what? We saw that video too. In fact, we had a whole training about it. We were told if a suspect refused to answer questions, we should call it resisting arrest. So, you are under arrest for resisting arrest. You have the right to remain silent. Anything you say can and will be used against you in a court of law. You have the right to an attorney. If you cannot afford an attorney, one will be provided for you. Do you understand the rights I have just read to you?"

I said nothing.

They said nothing.

I'm not sure I wouldn't rather they'd talked trash to me. I could hear the murderous rage that many cops might switch into when they meet defiance.

Silence all the way to Central Station. They handed me over to the booking clerk. With efficient professionalism, the dour woman in control took my fingerprints and my mug shot.

In the next room, tiled in yellow and white, two rookies, one Asian, the other Puerto Rican, both under twenty-five, flashed me sinister smiles. This job was probably some kind of initiation. The Asian cop held the spigot of the water pressure hose like a gun in his hand.

"Take your clothes off, sir," the Puerto Rican said.

I froze. Panties? Cock cage? What would they do with that?

They sighed as they approached me. They politely

removed my shirt. Unbuckled my pants. When the panties peeked out, they froze.

"What have we here?" the Asian cop said. "Panties. And what the hell is that thing on his dick?"

The other cop opened the door and hollered, "Hey, boys, come get a look at this!"

About half a dozen cops huddled in the doorway, erupting in general hilarity.

To my great horror, my penis hardened.

"Turn around," said the Asian cop, as if I was auditioning for his porn film.

"Look at this!" With my back to the audience, he lowered my panties and showed the stripes of Aletha's cane, the brand. "He must like it!"

One of the older white cops slapped his hand with his billy club. An obscene look on his face and a bulge in the crotch of his uniform.

"Bend over."

I did.

"Spread your cheeks."

In no position to argue, I pulled them wide.

He tapped the billy club on my ass. "I bet you like me to stick this up there, wouldn't you, Girly-boy?" But he just hit me across my ass cheeks.

"I got a better idea," he said. "Take his pretty panties off and wash him down, boys."

The Asian cop said, "What about that thing on his dick?"

The older guy looked at it. "Naw. I ain't touching that. Leave it on."

They pulled off my panties and plastered me with a high-pressure stream of hot water that nearly knocked me over. They threw me a towel, my panties, and an orange jump suit. "Put the panties back on, Girly-boy," the old guy said.

I tried to follow his order, but my hands were still cuffed. I nearly fell over. "Oh." The white guy removed my cuffs.

The jump suit had the back hatch missing, like a child's pajamas but without the buttoning flap, revealing my pantied butt.

The giggling entourage followed the white guy and me to the felony holding cell. The six inmates included a short, mean-looking Black guy with jail-house muscles and violent tattoos covering his arms and chest – snakes and death heads.

"Here's a present for you, boys." The cop threw me toward the mean-looking one and retreated, presumably to watch the action on the security cameras in each corner of the cell.

I sat down on the floor to cover my exposed panties. My cock was hard enough to complete the electric circuit – but Aletha must have turned off the device.

The Black man smirked at me. "They call me Redbone." He had a gravelly James Earl Jones Darth Vader voice. "Peter." My voice a squeak. I was about two feet from his bunk.

He smiled shyly. "You know they're giving you to me." His voice was soft.

"So I gathered."

"Don't worry, Peter. I may be a lot of things, but I'm no rapist. Plenty here would gladly rape you. Maybe you'd like that? But I got standing – I'm the fucking alpha dog, you dig?"

"Okay. Thanks, I think."

Redbone laughed. "You have a sense of humor."

"Got to."

"Got that right."

His voice was hypnotic. My body relaxed into its femininity, surrendering.

His presence in the cell was like a Plexiglas bubble surrounding him and me, protecting us from the others. A force field no one dared challenge.

He didn't rush me. He took his sweet time, a little slower than I wanted him to, to be honest.

It didn't hurt that I had utterly no choice.

"I know we're not supposed to ask, but what are you in for?" he asked. "We don't get many white boys in here."

"They're charging me with resisting arrest. There was a demonstration at the Supreme Court."

"I been following that. Those court cases."

"You?" I asked.

"Killed a guy. Another guy. Third one. Had to. It's kill or be killed out there, man."

In my trance, I burbled, "Yeah, I'm about to kill someone."

"What do you mean?"

"Nothing." I was terrified he would pursue it, so I moved closer to him, leaned against the side of his bunk in a languid way, still hiding my backside, but spreading my legs invitingly, not concerned about him seeing the bulge in my pants. He put his hand on my shoulder.

I was resigned – somewhat deliciously so – to letting this man have his way with me. His loneliness touched me.

One of the guards approached the cell and called my name. "Graves."

As I rose to follow the guard, I felt Redbone's eyes on my ass.

Aletha and Roger were standing in the family waiting area. They looked worried as if they were bailing out their teenage son picked up for loitering.

"Finally," she said. "What's with the outfit?" She was referring to the orange jump-suit with the cutout in the rear, like the Coppertone kid in the old ad.

I smiled and shrugged.

She called to the admittance clerk. "Can we get his clothes please?"

The woman brought out a plastic box.

Aletha and Roger stood around me, shielding the view from visiting family members the room while I changed.

"We bailed you out, Peter, so you belong to us. Again."

"I wasn't trying to escape you. I was in that tunnel by the Supreme Court so I couldn't answer your phone call."

They looked at each other. I'm not sure they believed me.

"Never mind. This is your big day, Pamela."

15

Be Prepared

Back at the dungeon, I effortlessly slipped into subspace. After the humiliation of being caught out by Matthew and Clarissa and then the cops and the jail, the distance between me and total selflessness was shrinking.

There was something else. I was surfing on the tide of history. Hours from now, I would make history. I would make a difference. I would have my meaningful death.

But did I really want to die? My headache from hell returned to remind that I was dying anyway. My cancer death would be slow and agonizing. My likely death at the hands of Justice Johnson's security detail would be swift.

I anticipated Aletha's and Roger's commands, so we went through the hours of preparation in complete silence, warm silence – I was theirs. I, Pamela, was an invention of Aletha and Roger. Peter was a willing collaborator.

I dropped to my knees and crawled after them into the bathroom. I removed my clothes, hung them on the back of the door. Roger and Aletha stood on each side of me, and we wrapped our arms around each other. They wore matching leather breeches, both of them topless. Aletha's breasts wrapped around my ribcage like pillows. Her wild corkscrew hair flamed my face.

"Breathe," she said. She knelt in front of me and, with a key that hung from her neck, she released the lock and removed my cock cage. My cock shot in the air with the rush of freedom Redbone would feel if suddenly released from prison.

"Oh, dear," she said and grabbed a wooden spoon hanging off the bathroom wall. She whacked my cock.

"How long since you've had an orgasm, Pamela?"

"Three weeks, Ma'am."

"Three weeks. What do you think, Roger? If we don't let her come now, as soon as she sees Johnson's cock, she'll spurt all over her panties. The Justice will want you to come when he fucks you in the ass, Pamela. Got that?"

"Yes, Ma'am."

"Okay," said Roger, in his calm, even, hypnotic voice. "Let's slow this way down. There's no hurry. Johnson won't be on his boat until tomorrow morning. We have until late tonight to get her ready. Plus, we want to have fun with her."

Aletha cackled with playful menace.

I retreated into deeper subspace to get beyond the headache, determined to enjoy my last few hours on earth.

Roger leaned me over Aletha's leather clad knee

and held my arm behind my back.

Swat. His hand on my ass. *Swat*. Pause. *Swat*. His inimitable rhythm making my ass quiver with anticipation. *Swat*.

Pushing on my bald head, Aletha forced me on my knees in the bathtub. She pulled a black four-quart enema bag off the wall. Filled it with warm water.

They massaged my buttocks, punctuated with occasional swats from Roger's hand.

Aletha covered her finger with Astroglide and greased up my ass, as well as the 18-inch colon tube. "Breathe," she whispered. She slowly slid the whole tube inside and released the flow, a tad warmer than room temperature.

My insides had not been so warm since I was back in the womb.

My belly distended. I cramped. I grunted. "Breathe!" she said.

I breathed.

She slowly pulled the tube out of me and with it came everything in my large intestine. My knees were soaked in the smelly mess.

I ejaculated without touching my penis.

"There you go, Pamela," Roger said. "You can thank us."

"Thank you, Sir. Thank you, Ma'am."

They filled me twice more. I would be pristine for the Justice.

"Clean this up, Pamela," Roger directed as they left.

I cleaned the tub with Comet. Thoroughly. I

cleaned my body with the Neutrogena Body Wash.

They returned to dry me off. Roger then spread Nair all over me, carefully avoiding my genitals, arm pits, and newly protruding nipples. Those other parts Aletha shaved expertly with a straight razor. Since taking the hormones, there wasn't nearly as much hair as there had been.

They had me wait ten minutes for the Nair to begin to burn, then they pushed me back in the shower and scrubbed me with a loofah – a rough tamale-shaped sponge.

They guided me, one on each arm, to the whipping bench. "You understand why you need to be whipped now?"

"Yes, Ma'am."

"It's to expiate the guilt ahead of time so you won't be bothered by your pacifist qualms when it comes to pulling the trigger. Pre-punishment makes you free."

I left my body quickly, watching from above as the countless strokes of the whip ravished my ass.

"Johnson believes that a well-dressed sissy must have a fresh set of welts on her ass," Aletha said.

Once I was released, Aletha sat me down at the dressing table and, with an arousing intimacy, did my toenails and finger nails in Pink Inferno.

Nails glistening, I was walked to the bureau and the closet.

"We want you to choose your outfit," Aletha said. "Remember, you will be on a yacht, so we're not doing evening gown here."

I chose lavender boycut panties, with matching bra, camisole, and garter belt. Aletha helped me
dress. She squeezed my budding titties and said,
"These will do, now, Pamela, congratulations! You
don't need the silicone breast forms." I slipped into
white fishnet stockings and covered my crotch just
barely with sand-washed cutoff jeans – hot pants
with rhinestone stars on the back pockets.

Aletha brought out a shoe box. "I just bought
these for you and Sylvester." From the tissue paper,
she pulled out pink, wedge platform high-top lace-up
sneakers. "Nice rubber soles so you won't slip on the
deck, Pamela."

She sat me at the dressing table and started on
my face.

She leaned my head back and shaved my face with
a straight razor like an accomplished barber, then
plastered my face with foundation. "Luckily Sylvester
likes his sissies on the old side. No idea why. Fetishes
have no rationale. He's about your age. You're fortu-
nate to have smooth skin, not all doughy like so many
older gentlemen – and ladies. Being bald makes the
wig work so much better, as well." She fitted a tight
wig cap, spread Pro Hair Ghost Bond wig glue around
the cap, and slid on the familiar Joan Baez wig which
still had the magenta tempera highlights.

"Here's how it will work, Pamela. You will stow
away on his boat after midnight. I have the key. You'll
be in the tight space under the cabin floorboards.

Hopefully, we've cured you of your claustrophobia. His security will come through around seven tomorrow morning. You will need to stop breathing for a minute or two."

Aletha plucked then darkened my eyebrows. She fattened my eyelashes with mascara.

"Johnson himself will hop on his boat at about eight AM. His security will follow in a motor boat. Except for his personal assistant Francisco, a short Filipino man who knows all about Johnson's dalliances and even facilitates them sometimes. Francisco will pilot the boat while you and Johnson play in the bedroom."

She added some violet eyeshadow. "You'll motor down the Potomac for several hours until you reach the Chesapeake. As soon as you're underway, you can extract yourself from the hold and crawl silently into the master stateroom. Wait there. Johnson will come to you when he's ready – after a couple of beers. It's his cover story for wanting to go to bed. Now the two of you can have your little orgy."

Grinning at the thought of me enjoying this encounter, she slammed my ball with her fist. She held my neck roughly while she rouged my lips with hot pink lipstick.

"Just before you get to the Bay itself, there's a secluded little cove where he likes to go. Francisco will weigh anchor in Palmer's Cove, and signal for the security boat to pick him up. He and Johnson still have a thing going, which requires being extra discreet by not having Francisco and Sylvester sleeping alone on the boat.

"Wait a discreet two hours. Snuggle with Sylvester. Nap a bit. Once it's good and dark, shed all your clothes but your shorts. Shoot him in the head. Put your phone in a Baggie. Then drop into the Bay and swim to shore. You can swim, can't you?"

"I can swim."

We were silent to let the instructions sink in.

"We want you to know we're behind you," Roger said. "We've got your back. Where you'll land on shore is in a secluded area of a park, Westmoreland State Park. No one around. We'll meet you. We'll track you on your phone and text you where to go when you reach shore.

"I also want you to know, Pamela, Peter," Roger continued," that personally I fully support what you're doing. Aletha has her personal reasons for wanting to take Sylvester out, but we both get the politics of it. Johnson could be the keystone of the Conservative movement. Like a Roman arch, it could collapse without him. Maybe. Maybe not. Did taking out Bin Laden destroy Al Qaeda? But every situation is different. This is a noble and significant thing you are doing, no matter what the outcome. There comes a point where you just have to throw shit against the wall and see what sticks. I think you'll stick."

"Thanks, I think."

"The pending reactionary cases will be postponed. After a period of mourning, the president will try to appoint another reactionary Black man – or woman – to

Sylvester's seat, but the Senate will block the appointment. A four-four court works in our favor. This is our hope, anyway. Lots could go wrong, of course. You could chicken out. You won't do that, will you, Pamela?"

"No, of course not. I've been waiting for this moment for a long time. I didn't imagine it would be done this way, but it works for me."

Roger pulled a gun out of the drawer in the dressing table. "This is a lady's gun, a .25 automatic. It's quiet, so Johnson's security probably won't hear the shots. Or shot. The best would be one shot to the temple. To make sure he's dead, you should fire another into his forehead."

He handed me the gun – smaller than my hand with a mother-of-pearl grip. I stuffed it in the pocket of my hot pants.

"If his security detail does hear the shots and you're caught?" Aletha said. "You're on your own. I recommend jumping in the water and trying to escape anyway. They'll shoot you. But you will have had a meaningful death. Isn't that what you wanted?"

I was quiet.

"If you surrender, there will be questions," she continued. "They will torture you in ways far less pleasurable than ours. It won't turn you on. Not even you, Sweetheart. You will be interrogated until you give us away. We can't have that. Open your mouth, Pamela."

Roger bent my head back and stuck something on one of my rear teeth.

"A cyanide capsule, Pamela. Just in case. It's in the back of your tooth now. If and when you need to use it, flip it down between your teeth with your finger and bite down hard. You'll be dead in five minutes.

"But the best scenario is for you to make it to shore. We'll meet you with arrangements to get to Venezuela."

I thought about that. "Venezuela. Could I go back to California instead? I miss my family."

"Haven't they pretty much disowned you?"

"I could win them back."

"We'll think about that," Aletha said. "It depends on how hot you are, if anyone saw you. We'll let you know when we pick you up. So there you are, Pamela. Let's have a look at you."

I stood up and pranced around with exaggerated movements, like the first dance of a stripper. I was feeling fully female as never before; at the same time about to commit murder. I comprehended that part of Aletha's genius was to transform me into a different person to get me beyond my ancient qualms. I wasn't Peter anymore. I was Pamela, and I was owned by Aletha, who had programmed me to fulfill my destiny.

Applause. "Looking good, if I say so myself." Aletha gloated. She embraced me in a long hug. There were tears in her eyes as she drew away. "Good luck, Pamela," she stage-whispered in her sexiest voice. "One more thing. Just in case things go south with Johnson." She handed me what looked like a tiny flash drive with a Velcro strip. "This is a video camera. See the tiny lens? As soon as you get into the stateroom on the yacht, install this baby in the bulkhead with the lens aimed at the bed. And don't forget to take it with you when you leave."

16

Pamela and the Justice

It was dark at 3 AM when they dropped me off in front of the Capital Yacht Club. Moonless. Aletha handed me two keys – one to the dock gate and one to *Supremacy*. "Once you're on the boat, go down to the bilge and hide in the crawl space. We'd take you, but a single white woman will attract much less attention than two Black people and a white woman."

I knew where the yacht was. I'd seen it. I let myself onto the pier and went straight to the big blue boat surrounded by the creaking of docks and mooring ropes straining against each wave.

This is it, I kept saying. My heart was aflutter like a school girl's – this deed was so, so wrong and at the same time so, so right.

I climbed onto the teak deck. The yacht groaned at my weight. I unlocked and relocked the door to the pilot room. By the head in the stern, I lifted the hatch, descended into the fiberglass keel, and pulled the hatch shut. I lay down to wait, crammed against the bare fiberglass of the hull, bumpy like spackled plaster, where it narrowed down into the keel. The bilge water smelled of milk gone sour.

I was sleepy, but too on edge to relax. I made sure the clip in the .25 automatic was full (6 shots) and installed. I'd never shot anyone before. A first time for everything. I was grateful to Aletha and Roger for programming me to not think about it. One shot to the temple, one to the forehead. I would feel exhilarated.

That I might actually get away with it had never occurred to me. Aletha and Roger would meet me on shore? Really? Would they take that risk for me? I liked the idea of living, even if just for a little while. To have a peek at the political shift.

The night was interminable. My consciousness seemed to descend into death. I was sure that as death approached, time slowed down. Way, way down. That the last nanosecond before you died could well last, experientially, as long as your natural life. And that decelerated time contained all of heaven and hell.

Would I suffer the fires of hell for this? Unlikely – too many lives would be saved by this single death. This single death could begin to reverse the direction of society. Not this act alone, of course. It would take the movement. But as Roger had said, Sylvester Johnson could be the keystone of the arch of corporate supremacy.

Or maybe this killing would be one more futile act in an infinite series of futile acts.

My whole body convulsed into tears. I was grieving my own death.

As the sobs subsided, my peephole of consciousness became unmoored, traveling to the plane where the battle against the cancer was raging. Except all was quiet – there seemed to have been a truce. Perhaps in anticipation of my real-life death.

And Frank, the mouse was with me. A representative of my karma, an early victim of my sinful mindlessness, my carelessness. My spirit guide to the underworld, the narrator of the life-long nanosecond of the end.

Frank's speck of consciousness spoke in a language of psychic understanding. "Welcome to the land of the dead, Peter. Stein and I will help you along the way." An amorphous stem cell transformed itself into another mouse, Stein.

"Hello again," Stein radiated. "We'll lead you down memory lane. You'll examine all your significant experiences, especially the ones like stomping of Frank and me. We are here to assure you of our forgiveness. You were young, and we were your best companions. You didn't mean to crush us. But you will still need to grieve your culpability, and forgive yourself. Like when you burned your cousin with a cigarette because you didn't want him at your party. Like when you dumped your girlfriend the same night her father died. This is just the introduction. We have sixty-some odd years to relive your life."

I must have finally dozed off. My peephole of consciousness snapped back into the bilge, startled by the clatter above me, Johnson's security detail going through the motions of checking out the boat.

I held my breath.

Quiet again. I waited until the grinding of the engine ripped through the hold, loud as the inside of a diesel semi's muffler.

I pushed up the hatch. All clear. I pulled myself up into the salon by the head and tiptoed to the master stateroom.

In a closet by the door of the stateroom was another head, an older model with a three-foot lead-pipe handle for pump-flushing. I quietly pissed in it. When I pulled, the handle came off in my hand. I stuck it back in its bracket, gave it a few more pumps.

I positioned the Velcro tape on the bulkhead and attached the tiny camera, then I slid into the softness of the queen-sized bed. I fell sound asleep.

When I opened my eyes, he was staring me, smiling, a mixture of sweetness and lasciviousness. He was a dark-skinned man, with a square jaw and smooth skin. His hair was cut medium short, not the semi-bald look in vogue among many younger Black men like the former president. There was just a hint of grey at his temples. His eyes were black and penetrating, as if he could see more than he let on. He was wearing a sky-blue polo shirt and green and yellow plaid Bermuda shorts. Stylishly retro. Brown leather Topsiders, no socks.

The power in his stance sent me into female subspace. I looked back at him sleepily, languidly, and smiled seductively, folding back the covers so he could get a good look at the merchandise. I felt deliciously like the whore that I was.

"Good morning, Pamela." His voice was soft and grainy. I could practically smell his arousal. Given the complexity of the arrangements, such trysts could not have been that frequent. "Mimosa?" He handed me a plastic champagne flute filled with vodka-spiked orange juice.

"Thank you, Sir."

"Perfect." His appraisal. His eagerness was almost embarrassing. We clunked our plastic glasses. I watched the tension in his muscles ease as he slowed himself down.

I could see the bulge in his shorts. I went full Mae West: "Is that a gun in your pocket or are you just happy to see me?"

He laughed. "A smartass. I like that."

It came to me suddenly: this was a Justice of the Supreme Court of the United States, one of the most powerful men in the world. Slobbering all over me.

"We've got time, Pamela. Plenty of time. Let's take it real slow, okay?" He seemed to be talking to himself. "Aletha's still got it. She knows what I like." He reached over and pushed a button on his phone blue-toothed into a speaker system. Norah Jones. *Waiting for you to come on home and turn me on... like a desert waiting for the rain.*

We like the same music?

I smiled, breathing into my surrender and spreading my legs to show off the bulge in my hot pants. "And I'm all yours."

"I'm forgetting my manners – you must be famished, stuck in the hold all that time." He reached into the small fridge, which also smelled of sour milk, and pulled out a plastic container. He portioned out the contents onto two small paper plates. "Ceviche. Spicy raw fish. As strong an aphrodisiac as raw oysters." He stuck a small fork in the mound of fish. I gobbled it quickly. I was famished. Didn't mind that it tasted like it was a ways beyond the expiration date.

"I was thinking we should talk first, get to know each other, but, I'm sorry, it's been too long."

"For me too."

"Stand up for me, Pamela."

I stood in front of him, my crotch inches from his face, and cocked my hips at him.

He sucked in his breath. "My, my, my. Turn around for me, dear."

I turned ever so slowly, swinging my hips like a cheap stripper.

"You are one hot cunt, Pamela."

"Yes, Sir."

"Kneel before me, Pamela."

"Yes, Sir." I knelt, and looked hungrily into his eyes, as if I was craving his dominance. Which I was.

He pushed my face into his crotch, his hard cock against my cheek. He reached into a large black bag and pulled out a heavy leather collar and strapped it around my neck. "You are mine now, Pamela." His voice sultry and even, approaching Roger's hypnotic tone. "I can do anything I want to you."

"Yes, Sir. Your wish is my command."

He stroked my head with surprising gentleness. "Anything." He ran his fingers down my face.

I took his forefinger into my mouth and lovingly sucked it.

He ran his hands inside my silky lavender camisole.

I stroked his thigh.

His arm reached down my back, under my shorts and panties, running his forefinger into the node at the base of my spine just where the crack in my ass began.

"Have you been a bad girl, Pamela?"

"Yes," I whispered emphatically, intuiting where this was going. Right where I wanted it to. "Yes, Sir. A very, very bad girl, I'm afraid." I glanced at his face and caught the gleam in his eye.

"Lower your shorts, Pamela."

I stood up to loosen them, exposing my lavender panties and matching garter belt. My shorts dropped to the floor and clunked with the weight of the gun. I prayed he didn't notice.

"Lie down on my lap, Pamela."

I complied. He lowered my panties. "Nice marks, Pamela. You are a well-dressed sissy slut." He started off with gentle warming slaps, alternating cheeks. Each stroke was harder than the last until my ass must have been a deep red and I started squealing with each blow. He stopped. "Breathe, Pamela." A moment of silence.

"I want you to suck my cock now, girl."

I lowered myself to my knees, unbuckled his belt.

Unbuttoned his Bermuda shorts. Pulled his black silk jockey shorts down to his knees and smiled. His erection wasn't long, but it was thick. I cupped his balls in my hand – Wait! He had only one ball! *What the fuck?* I slowly lowered my mouth around his cock, carefully pouting my lips so he wouldn't feel my teeth. I closed my eyes and slipped into deep subspace, where all my awareness was filled with the sucking of the Justice's cock. I opened my throat, suppressed a gag. Shivered as though I would have a full mouth orgasm like Linda Lovelace.

"You're a good little cocksucker, Pamela." A sultry whisper. He grabbed my cock and squeezed my ball. "She got to you, too!"

"But, you?"

"I used to be a sub, visited Aletha maybe four times a year. Something about her cutting off my ball and making me eat it – I suddenly switched. Next visit, I tied her up and beat the shit out of her. So she trained me to work as a Dom with her sissy boys, and I liked it. From the bottom to the top. Without that I'd never have arrived at the top of the social food chain. It's ironic – give up a ball to get balls. Now I'm one of the most powerful ballers on Earth.

"I don't feel it though. I feel like the little boy simpering as my father whips me with his heavy leather belt.

"Now I want to whip your ass, Pamela. and fuck you. Take the rest of your clothes off." Deborah Cox shimmied from the speakers, "Nobody's Supposed to Be Here."

"We like the same music," I said.

I sensually slipped out of the camisole, the bra, the panties, the garter belt, the stockings.

He reached into his bag and strapped the leather cuffs to my wrists and ankles. He patted the center of the bed.

"Assume the position, my perfect Pamela," he said and I crawled to the center of the bed on my knees with my ass in the air. He locked me in position.

He began with a flogger, switched to a riding crop, then to a rattan cane. I dug into subspace, his rabid intensity reached my depths. I screamed.

He snapped a ball gag into my mouth and whipped some more.

In another breath, he unsnapped me and un-gagged me, tore off his shirt and shorts, slipped under me and pulled me onto his nakedness. Lying side by side, our cocks electrified by their contact, our rigid nipples pressed against each other. He kissed me – a lover's kiss, with a gentle tongue.

Millie Jackson's "Slow Tongue" enveloped us from the speaker.

He felt my body, stroked me all over, throbbing toward the brink. He read my mind, or my body. "You may not come, Pamela. I will come first inside you. But I have many more plans for you. I want this to last. Who knows when I'll have another chance to ravish such a beauty." We made out like a couple of teenagers.

"Time to assume the position again, Pamela."

He knelt behind me, his cock pressing against my ass crack. "Open for me, Sesame." He stroked the cheeks, swatted them, used gobs of warm Astroglide to grease up my sissy cunt. He inserted one finger. Two fingers. Three fingers.

Then his cock. No condom, but STDs were not high on my worry list given the circumstances. He entered slowly, squeezing my hormone swollen tits. All motion stopped. "Feel me, Pamela. Feel me."

Three slow slides and he spasmed to orgasm. An animal in its death throes.

I stretched out, the Justice still inside me. We may have even dozed off.

"It's your turn, Pamela." He snapped the cuffs to the eyelet at each corner of the bed , spread-eagling me face up and crouched on his knees between my legs. He lubed and stroked my penis. "You're not allowed to come yet, Pamela." I was about to involuntarily disobey him when a wooden spoon slapped my cock.

He looked at me admiringly. "I know Aletha sent you to kill me."

My body stiffened and pulled against the restraints. *Oh, shit.* Everybody's last words.

He fished my hot pants from the floor and extracted the .25 automatic. "I thought you were cool until that clunk. I'm sorry you missed your chance. Why didn't you kill me right away?"

I knew I sounded desperate. "I had the gun for protection. How could I know what to expect, in *flagrante delicto* with a powerful man of justice whose view of the world is diametrically opposed to mine?"

"Yeah, right, Pamela. You forget I know Aletha. I was wondering why she agreed to hook us up. Time for a little honesty. I was too desperate for the likes of your sweet nooky to care. Sex addicts take risks. Did you know that? So now, what are we going to do with you?"

"Let me go and call it even?"

"But I have the upper hand now. I could kill you in the worst, most painful way possible. It would be the most exquisite orgasm imaginable. Worth every penny I gave Aletha." I squirmed against my restraints.

"Regrettably I'm not sure I have the stomach for killing. You may be in luck."

My mind sharpened, as if someone had just tripled the ROM in my brain. Stomach or no, he could still kill me. So much for my meaningful death. No one would ever know except Aletha and Roger. And they would never tell.

"Have you ever killed anyone?" I asked.

"You mean besides those murderers I cleared for execution?" He sneered, mocking my politics. "No. You will be my first."

"You'd be doing me a favor, really. I've got this nasty brain cancer, diffuse astrocytoma. I'm ready to die."

A tiny mouse-voice deep in my brain squeaked, "Are you?"

Sylvester continued in a judicial way. "One problem is I kind of like you, Pamela. We're not that different. We both want people to be happy."

"There's a big difference, Sir," I foolishly argued. "I believe in compassion for my fellow humans. You, Sir, are a victim of compassion fatigue. Or worse – you have a congenital compassion deficit. You deny poor people the slightest relief."

He frowned. I might have touched a nerve. "I have compassion for you."

"Do you?"

"Have you done much with knives?"

"No." I hoped my tone conveyed that I really wasn't into that. At least not yet. Sylvester pulled a leather covered wooden box out of his black bag. Something worthy of a chef's fine cutlery. He displayed the set of gleaming, scalpel-like knives.

"Don't worry, they're fully sterilized. Though I'm not sure if that will make that much difference."

He started to cut, to make little tiny slits on my tits, chest, and belly. Sharp pricks. He moved down to my hips, a few pricks in my prick, on down to the thighs. The blood was minimal. No more than popping pimples.

"I see you like this." He rubbed his hand on my erect cock. "We'll see how much it turns you on to be cut in little pieces and fed you to the sharks, Chum. Get it, Chum?"

"That is beyond my limits, Sir."

He laughed. He got my joke. "Limits? What Limits? You came here to kill me. There are no limits to the quantity of pain you will suffer for what you were too weak to pull off. I wonder what it's like to flay someone alive. Of course I'll cauterize the wounds with a butane torch so you don't mess up the bed."

I discovered that the shallow immediacy of fear obstructed the diffuse depths of subspace, but cutting drew the justice into his own trance, as he code-switched to Black English. "Some of your white honky liberals fought racism in a bad-ass way, man. Suffered for helping Blacks. Schwerner. John Brown. Plenty of others. But most of them wasn't willin to die for the cause. They thinks they stand against racism gives them some kinda pass to be even more racist. They thinks the fact that they fought for us Negroes – and some of them motherfuckers fought damn hard, harder than most Blacks – that give them the damn mojo to tell us what to do. Johnson – that's President Johnson, no relation far as I know – you got to hand it to the old cracker. He was able to see how cool it was to embrace King (holding his nose, you know) and pass the Civil Rights and Voting Rights Acts."

His knife was precise, relentless, punctuating his sermon.

"War on poverty, she-it. Even a knee-jerk like you can see that welfare is a cruel drug, just like all the drugs the welfare supports. It's one picture, one whole piece, you dig? Welfare a damn subsidy for the drug lords. I can say that. I might get attacked, but it's true, ain't it? Same old fuckin story. The whites feels like they give Blacks something – they think they ain't racist no more, so they gets to act out racism big time. Johnson could do all that for "us," then turn round and drop fire on the gooks of Vietnam. I was against that war, dig? But I ain't naïve. Johnson hisself said it best. 'They want what we have and we're not going to give it to them.'"

"I remember that from your memoir, Sir."

"You read it? I won't ask what you thought. You reek of liberal bias, like rotten chitlins."

"It wasn't bad, your book. A lot I don't agree with, but you come off as real."

He switched knives – a long skinny one for cutting neck to butt. Two inches apart. I waited for the crosscut making me perfect bait for the bull sharks that occasionally cruise Chesapeake Bay.

"Yeah, man, I real all right. Y'know Malcolm told us we was chumps to give all our support to one party, the damn Dixiecrats. In the Democrat Party, I'm just one more nigger easy to stonewall. But hey, check this out, in the Republican Party I'm the hot-shit nigger, voice of the damn people. I get that I got on the big Court cuz they gotta fill the Black seat and I'm the only nigger lawyer they know. Big surprise to me when they pick me, but then I hear they been groomin me for this some twenty years.

"So Pamela, you motherfuckers have no idea what shit go down in DC. It sure as fuck ain't about no democracy, I'll tell you that. Black people *never* had no fucking democracy. This song-and-dance that you guys pour your damn hearts into – Congress, POTUS, SCOTUS, you only seein the tip of the damn cotton ball. There's a whole nother government, and it ain't really a secret.

The fucking National Security State, brother, welcome to it, the folks with the weapons who calls the shots. NSA, CIA, FBI. Homeland security. Secret Service. Army, Navy, Air Force, Marines. They don't give a fuck about no elections. They got shit on everyone and they ain't scared to use it. Thank one J. Edgar Hoover for this shit. That motherfucker had more power than the presidents even with old-school intelligence tools. Until they caught him dressed like you anyway."

While endorphins battled the pain, my gut spoke up, convulsing as though he'd punched me in it.

"Excuse me, Sir. Hold that thought. Your ceviche is working its revenge. I got a serious urge to shit. I'm afraid of messing your bed."

He sighed and looked at me, suspicious. A juicy gurgle dribbled from my ass.

"Okay. I hate shit all over my sheets. How does that go? I slit a sheet, a sheet I slit, upon the slitted sheet I sit." He clipped a rhinestone-studded leash to my collar before unsnapping my wrists and ankles and led me toward the head.

My gut exploded in the toilet, despite yesterday's enema. Fear and fish toxins – a bad combo. He held the leash and watched me shit.

This was my chance. My only chance. Though I'd never even seen a Bruce Lee film, I torqued the handle of the head flushing pump and sprang at him like a mountain lion, slamming the pump handle onto his head with all my might. He staggered the three steps back to the bed.

I thought he was out, but I smashed his head again, then grabbed the gun out from where he'd stashed it.

I aimed as instructed. *Now!* I could hear Aletha say. *Now!*

I couldn't do it. A cosmic ache filled my head. I heard a mouse squeak, "No."

With shaking hands, I spread-eagled him across the bed and tied his wrists and ankles. His head was bleeding. Blindfolding him, I smeared his blood on my hands.

I ripped off the video camera and stuck it in my pants with the gun and my phone.

I wasn't sure what I wanted, but I didn't want to waste time. Since he was still breathing, I filled a pitcher with water, threw in some ice, shook it up and dumped it on his head.

"Turnabout is fair play," he said groggily. "Nicely played, Pamela."

"Thank you, Sir."

"But I can't see your luscious ass. Fuck, I think I'm blind. "

"Sorry, Sir. It was an accident committed in self-defense."

"You didn't kill me while you had the chance."

"And you didn't kill me when you had the chance."

"Big mistake on both our parts."

"Maybe. But now I have another chance. I can wait until Francisco leaves the boat. I might just get away."

"I suppose. It will be awhile. I could scream his name now. Then you'd have to kill him too. How can you kill two men if you don't have the guts to kill one?"

I reached for the gag.

"Don't bother. I won't yell. I'd feel terrible if you did get the nerve and shot poor Francisco."

I lay down on my back with my head resting in his crotch. "Let's talk about the court cases," I said.

"What about them?"

"The four of them coming before the court. The one in Florida even taking voting rights from people with two misdemeanors. Merely misdemeanors, Sylvester, not felonies. As a Black man, you know that's unfair."

"Granted it's a sleazy transparent ploy to reduce the Democrat vote and keep conservatives in power. But that's a good thing for the country. Besides, how many of these people would actually vote anyway?"

"So the decision won't make much difference?"

"Probably not – beyond showing who's in charge. Anyway, I'm up there with Newt – It's too god damn expensive to keep all those minor offenders in jail."

"Okay. What about abortion?"

"I'm of mixed minds. Rape is sticky, of course. You have to admit it might not be the woman's fault. And all around me growing up I saw that poor people have too many babies, reinforcing their poverty."

"So there's wiggle room there?"

Silence. He seemed to see where my line of inquisition was going.

"Carbon. Shouldn't the government be able to regulate carbon emissions? You're not a dyed-in-the-wool climate change denier, are you?"

"I'm not blind, Pamela – except right at this moment – climate change is real, and it's caused by human activity, and no you may not quote me on that. But what about China, Russia, and India? They're spewing tons more shit in the air than we are. We can't put ourselves at a competitive disadvantage."

"Ever consider that we might *all* lose the race? Your race, my race, the human race? Okay, one more. The Coalition of Cancer Cooperatives wants to use fresh strains of embryonic stem cells in developing cancer treatments. This one matters to me, Sylvester. These stem cells could save my life."

"Creating embryos only to kill them sets a bad precedent. When you make it so personal, I suppose I don't feel that strongly about it."

"You really are a reactionary bastard, aren't you, Sylvester? Can I call you Sylvester?"

"You hold the gun. I guess you can call me anything you like."

"I do hold the gun. And I'm coming to a firm decision here, now that we've fully switched. Think Aletha's surgery will make me a Dom, too? I'm going to stick to the plan. I'm going to kill you. As soon as Francisco leaves the boat."

"Unless," he said.

"Unless what?"

"What if I agreed to recuse myself on these four cases?"

"Really? You would do that?"

"If it would save my life. My own base might kill me later. If I just didn't vote, each case would result in a tie vote, and the rulings of the lower courts would stand. Rulings that in each case were in your favor."

"I guess I could ensure that by keeping you tied up here until the cases come before the court next week. Even if you assured me you wouldn't vote, how could I enforce that?" I was riffing, thinking out loud. "I do have the rights to blackmail," I said. "More effective coming from me than from Aletha. I'm white and still male enough. And you can't get the CIA to fire *me*. I have nothing to lose."

"There's my word. I've sworn an oath of office."

"Like everyone else in Washington, Sylvester, that and $6.00 will buy you a latte."

I brandished the camera. "I know you can't see, but my little video camera recorded everything that went on in here. Consider it my insurance policy. If all else fails, both our visages, let alone asses and dicks, will be all over xhamster.com. I've already lost everything but half my manhood. You've got more on the line."

Sylvester pleaded as if I'd stabbed him. "Pamela, please don't give the video to Aletha," he whined. "For some reason, I trust you to adhere to our agreement. But her? She'll be pissed as hell that you didn't kill me. She'd like nothing better than seeing me on xhamster. Except maybe money. She'll try for money.

If I gave her the money, she'd post the video anyway."

"To be fair, Mr. Justice, you may be misjudging my mentor."

The engine died. We must have arrived at the cove and weighed anchor.

I was wondering what to do next. Torturing him with polemic sounded fun. Whipping him with words gave me a hard-on.

I rummaged through his toy bag. *Perfect*. A cock cage with a remotely activated tens unit. I laughed.

I locked it on him. Humming to myself like some mad tinkerer. The way Leonardo must have hummed as he was inventing the tank.

I tested it. The justice's dick jerked into the air. It worked. I set it on pulse to send a stiff jolt about every 30 seconds.

"It said in your memoir that in your college years you were sympathetic to the Panthers. What made you change your mind?"

"You know Garvey was a pretty conservative guy. I admired the Black Muslims, too – for their self-help philosophy, for rehabilitating criminals and drug addicts by convincing them to hate Whitey. It's not like Whitey didn't deserve to be hated.

"It's funny, Pamela. I feel like I can be completely honest with you, as I've never been with anyone before. Certainly not my wife. She knows about this stuff without knowing. She silently cuts me slack around it – not without disdain. What do I have to hide from you? You're probably going to kill me anyway."

His body spasmed from the jolt.

"Ow!" He continued, "So what the fuck? Garvey hooked up with the KKK. He understood that they were the true representatives of the white race. Those whites who distanced themselves from the KKK were just liars. They felt the same way. So, Garvey-KKK, Hitler-Stalin, Sylvester Johnson-Ronald Reagan.

"What do you want, Pamela? Suppose I arrange a heart attack and sit out the session. You get your criminal votes, your abortions, your carbon restrictions, your stem cells. Do you think it will make much difference, Pamela?"

"Maybe not just these four votes. If you were dead, I think it could turn the tide."

"Turn the tide. What does that even mean? Ow!" Another jolt.

"The president will appoint another reactionary, but the Senate won't confirm him or her. The right-wing majority will be broken. Citizen's United will be overturned. The stranglehold on democracy since Bush v. Gore will be broken."

"That one was a doozy, I grant you."

"Will the four cases next week make all the difference? No. but the people's movement will be handed a great victory, which will hopefully result in its dramatic growth."

"You are some kind of fucking socialist."

"I'm not any kind of ismist. I want people to have more than just equality of opportunity. I want them to have equality, period. Take all the wealth in the world and divide it up equally among the seven plus billion people."

"A communist then! I can't believe I fucked a communist!"

"I'll wash your dick if you ask politely. I probably can't convince you to abandon your reactionary politics, but I can do this." I turned the remote three-quarters toward max. Sylvester's body danced, vibrated, levitated off the bed. He screamed. A full-bodied masculine scream. I slapped the gag on him and turned tens unit off.

I removed the gag. "You like that?"

"No."

"This could work, then. I'll be in court on the day that the four cases are decided. If you vote the wrong way, you get shocked until you keel over. The doctors will discover the cock cage, and you will have some explaining to do."

"You've got the power, Pamela."

"Don't give in too easily, Sylvester, I won't believe you." I turned on the remote full blast, gagged Sylvester again, and left it on until he passed out.

My erection demanded action. Ice-water over his head woke him. I squatted over Sylvester's mouth and removed the gag. "Open, sesame," I commanded and dropped my ball into his mouth. "Hum, Sylvester, hum."

He hummed.

I turned around and sat on his face. "Lick my ass, Sylvester. Stick your tongue all the way in there. Eat my shit."

My cock in his mouth choked him beyond a gag reflex. I fucked his face until I spurted my cum down his throat.

Just at that moment there was a knock at the door, like a signal, bom-ta-bom-ta-bom-bom. I held up the remote to threaten Sylvester into silence.

"That's Francisco's signal. He's leaving. He'll be on the security boat."

Dusk was settling in. In the mahogany galley, I explored the smelly fridge. I found some Italian salami and smoked Gouda cheese with a little mold on it. I trimmed off the mold and returned to the bed, filling both of our mouths with salami and cheese.

I lay with my head in his crotch, waiting for the dark. We were silent. If I accomplished my goal with these four critical cases, why not control him forever?

Of course he could have the cock cage removed – Francisco would arrange it discreetly. But would he? Why didn't I have the cage removed when Aletha had control over me? Because I liked it.

If the plan worked, I could be back in Oakland within a month to live out my life. Would Mariana take me back? Would Aletha let me go, unhappy that I didn't complete my mission?

Maybe it was an endorfinated illusion, but because we had shared both giving and receiving pain, the link between Sylvester and me felt potent – perhaps more powerful than the United States Supreme Court. Or the United States of America for that matter.

Sylvester was crying. I'm a dacryphiliac, among other things. I get a hard on when I see people cry. I moved in on him, my erect cock against his cock cage. As I took to the top, I shuddered. A burst of energy surged through me, like a shock from the cock cage. But different. This was *dominant* energy. This was power. I was lying on top of a Justice of the United States Supreme Court.

I kissed his tears.

In a soft, little boy voice, he said, "If we get through this in one piece, I'd like to see you from time to time." Not something this man told all the girls.

If we get through this.

"You are one hell of a negotiator, Pamela."

"Thank you, Sylvester. I'm sensing we reached a deal. Nothing in writing – this encounter between us never happened."

"Of course," Sylvester said.

"I let you go and swim to shore with my iPhone wrapped in plastic. You'll recuse yourself, so that the lower court ruling stands in each case."

His silence unnerved me. Finally, with a Buddha smile and a voice encompassing grief and joy, he said, "Yes, Sir."

I laughed. We kissed.

A velvet moonless dark had descended over the cove. To reinforce the deal and kill time until it was safe for me to swim ashore, I removed his cock cage and gave him a long, slow hand job, generously slathering his cock, balls, and asshole with Astroglide, dancing my fingers in and out of him until he came again. "Good boy," I said. I locked his cock back in the cage and hung the key around my neck.

Before dressing, I used Sylvester's silk boxer shorts to wipe the small bits of blood from the little cuts. I looked like I had a mild case of chicken pox. But the lacerations would heal quickly.

I donned panties, hot pants, lavender camisole and left off the garter belt and stockings. It would be hard to swim in my high-heel sneakers, but harder to walk without them. I tied the laces around my waist.

I snapped a photo of the IP address on the tens-unit so I could download the app that controlled it.

The gun, iPhone, and video camera were safely sealed in the zip-lock Baggie and stuffed in my pocket.

"So, we're good, Sylvester, right?" He remained spread-eagled and blind-folded on the bed as I stood over him with my hand on my hip and my hip cocked toward him. I needed one more confirmation.

"We're good, Pamela."

I kissed him on the lips and gave his ball a squeeze. I loosened the rope on his right hand, without untying it. With some wriggling, he could get his hand loose and get dressed before Francisco returned in the morning.

I shot up the stairs onto the deck. A salty haze covered the stars. The moon was new. The only light came from his security detail's boat a hundred yards away. The shore was maybe 500 yards away, a bit of a swim. But I knew better than to hesitate. I dove in and swam as if my life depended on it, which it did.

17

Betrayal

I landed on the stony beach of Westmoreland State Park. I waited 45 minutes for Aletha and Roger. I was hardly surprised that they didn't show. I tried phoning but had no service. I trekked through the woods. Something in my connection with Sylvester told me that Aletha would be mad. She'd want to beat the shit out of me for sure. But she probably wouldn't kill me.

It was after midnight when I found the two-lane road. Wet and androgynous, make-up hopelessly smeared, I stuck out my thumb.

A bearded guy in an old Ford pick-up stopped. He seemed friendly – a Grateful Dead type, complete with lightning bolt skull on his t-shirt, driving barefoot.

I asked him to drop me somewhere where I could catch a bus or a train back to DC. But why go back to DC? All I had there is very pissed off dominatrix and a submissive Supreme Court Justice who would do what he's told. But I had to be near enough to him to enforce our contract.

"Rough night?" he asked.

"That would be an understatement."

He took me all the way to Huntington, the last station on the Yellow Line of the Metro. The Metro app on my phone let me charge my fare.

It was peaceful back at the Hotel Manolo. I hadn't sensed I was being followed on the subway. My room didn't feel like it was under surveillance – though I suspected it was. I felt safe.

I connected my phone to the charger and snapped the cyanide capsule into the toilet. In the mirror, I looked as if I had jailbird stripes tattooed on my body from the cuts. I rubbed off the make-up and treated myself to a long, hot shower. The aftershocks of my yachting excursion began to wane.

I called Mariana. It would be about midnight on the west coast.

"Peter!" she screamed in a voice that gave me hope.

"Hi."

"How are you? Where are you? What are you doing?"

"Talking to you on the phone, Babe." It had been a while since I called her that.

"Always the jokester."

"That's me."

"So? What do you want?"

"I ask myself the same question."

"Enough with the jokes."

"I just persuaded Supreme Court Justice Sylvester Johnson to recuse himself from the four court decisions. I didn't have to kill him."

"Really?" Abrupt shift of tone. "And how did you do that?"

"It's a long story."

"I bet it is," her voice reverting to disdainful, tired of my stories. Tired of me. Ouch.

"You'll see in a few days when they start handing down the decisions."

"Uh huh."

"Afterward, I'd like to come home. To you. To our home."

"Uh huh."

"What does that mean?"

"I kind of like things the way they are, Peter." Her voice did crack a little. She wasn't enjoying letting me down. "You might want to get some help. You still have health insurance. You sound a little...distraught."

"Oh." Sniffles on the other end – no, on both ends. I was crying myself. In fact, I was sobbing so hard I whispered "I'm sorry" and hung up. I let the tears come. My body convulsed in grief – this was the moment I understood that it was over between Mariana and I. Viscerally.

I lay naked on top of the bed, conjuring the images of myself and Sylvester spread-eagled on the stateroom bed, as well as the DaVinci drawing of Man. I awoke at 9 AM.

I called Matthew. He reported that the city was in a frenzy with everyone was expecting riots after the Supreme Court's reactionary rulings. Our movement was planning to encircle the White House, the

Capitol, the Supreme Court building, and the Mall – the very seat of government – before the verdict. What to do next wasn't planned yet. Oh, and I'd been indicted along with eight others of the phony Supreme Court judges for "impersonating a federal official" and "defiling a government office" – a law stemming from the Berrigan brothers pouring blood on draft files. No one had been arrested yet, but rumors were rampant. They wanted the leaders off the street as soon as the decisions came down.

"We're meeting the night before the verdict, tomorrow night, at the Unitarian Church."

"Is that a good idea to have all the leaders in one place like that?" *Or to be telling me over the phone, for that matter.*

"They won't arrest us before the verdict goes down. It would look bad, like prior restraint."

"Extraordinary situations force people to act in extraordinary ways. Anyway, I'm pretty sure all the decisions will go our way. I can't tell you how I know this, I just do."

"Really, Peter? What have you been smoking?"

I told him I would try to be at the meeting. As any organizer worth his salt knows, yes means maybe, "I'll try" means no.

I wondered about Aletha. She'd be waiting for the news that Justice Johnson was dead. She must have an inkling by now that I had failed in my mission. What would she be thinking now? Revenge, of course. I figured I had about twelve hours before she would be after me. But I had to remain at large in order to be at the courthouse to enforce my contract with Johnson.

I suddenly thought of my burner phone and those other boys, Thing One and Thing Two. I pulled it out of the drawer and glanced at it: 27 messages. They might not be happy either.

It occurred to me that I should move, that I should splurge on a room at the Hilton or somewhere to keep myself safe until the court session was over.

As I began contracting my limbs to move into action, the door slammed open. "Freeze!" Thing One and Thing Two, guns drawn, shouted in unison.

I froze.

"Get dressed. We're taking you in."

"For what?"

"Suspected terrorism."

"Oh."

I took my time to dressing, carefully picking out frilly deep purple panties, sashaying my hips as I pulled them on. I smiled at the boys. I covered them with the spandex bicycler's outfit that Aletha had approved as sufficiently androgynous – black and yellow triangles orbiting red rectangles.

I made them wait while I brushed my teeth.

Once I was ready, they each took an arm, man-rushed me downstairs, and threw me in the back of the black Fairlane with the darkened windows.

They took me to the same concrete basement, sat me at a grey metal table. They looked ready for a long night.

"Here's the deal, Peter. You know you've been in-dicted with the rest of what your people are calling the Supreme Court 9. We need to be able to arrest your comrades, but they have been eluding our surveil-lance. We need your help," said the fat one, Thing One.

They thought I would give up my comrades just like that? What kind of a pussy did they take me for? They forgot – I can take torture.

"Why should I help you?"

"Because you have no choice. We will keep you here until you spill the beans," said Thing Two.

Is that all? Still, I did have a problem. With the first decision due in less than 48 hours, I needed to get the timing right on Sylvester's shocks.

With eight people besides me headed for the church tomorrow, surely there was some surveil-lance. So I wouldn't be giving anything away, would I?

"Can you get me into the courtroom for when SCOTUS hands down their decision?"

"Why?" asked Thing One.

"To witness history. For the book I'm writing."

"Oh, yeah, about murdering a Supreme Court Justice."

I was quiet.

"If you've got something for us, that might be arranged."

"Might be? I'm not good with probabilities."

"Okay," said Thing Two. "We will arrange that."

"Is that a promise?"

"That's a promise."

I hesitated, then sucked in my breath. "There's a meeting tomorrow night."

Thing One and Thing Two brightened. "Where?"

"All Souls Unitarian Church on 16th."

"Really? What time?"

"About 6, I think. We're all supposed to be there."

"Thank you, Peter. That's helpful."

"May I leave now?"

"We need to verify, of course. What if it turns out you're lying?" said Thing One. "We'll let you go as soon as our surveillance tells us the meeting is actually taking place."

"You will arrest them all?"

"We can't tell you that."

"So I'm stuck here for 24 hours?"

"I'm afraid so, Peter. But you're our friend now. We'll treat you right. No dark closets. We'll get you a cot. And a nice meal. What would you like to eat?"

"Filet mignon, baked potato with sour cream and chives, asparagus with Hollandaise sauce," I joked.

"You got it, buddy!" said Thing Two.

I felt as if I'd just ordered my last meal.

18

Switch

It was for the greater good, I kept telling myself. They would have been caught anyway. I did not feel good about having given up my comrades. I felt bad about it. So bad I couldn't sleep, despite sleeping being one of my consummate skills. I kept wondering if they'd find out that I had betrayed them – though it would be pretty obvious, me being the only one who wasn't at the meeting and the only one not arrested. Still, it would all be clear when the decisions came down on the side of the people. Wouldn't it?

The next night about 7:00, Thing One and Thing Two returned, beaming. "Your intelligence checked out, Peter," said Thing One. "All eight of leaders have been arrested. Congratulations."

My heart sank.

"You're free to go now, buddy," said Thing Two. He handed me a red paper tag with the number 1 printed on it. "This will get you into the courtroom, first of all the visitors, but you better go early."

I walked out of the nondescript unmarked office building not knowing where I was. Somewhere in the massive infrastructure of the federal bureaucracy.

Walking past one ugly dark grey building after another, I finally wondered into L'Enfant Plaza, a huge shopping-office center. I hopped down into the Metro, anxious about being seen either by movement people who knew I'd betrayed them – or by Aletha and Roger who by now would know I had failed in my mission.

I checked my phone for a hotel. The Capital Hill Hotel was $135 a night, three blocks from the court. One stop away on the Blue Line.

I breathed in luxury as I checked in. A pleasant room with a king size bed. Took a long shower, ordered an artisan pizza from room service, and watched Fox News wax ecstatic over the arrest of "suspected terrorists" at the Unitarian Church.

I lay naked and spread-eagled on the bed. I deserved a little luxury.

The inimitable plastic click of the hotel door. *Of course they found me.* Surprised but not surprised. Dressed in leather – she in the many-buttoned shirt-dress and boots, he with the pants, the vest.

They stared down at me with unmitigated fury. Silence. Roger hog-tied me with nylon rope, my ass bared to fate.

Well-choreographed whipping – Aletha with a cat o' nine tails, Roger with a snake whip.

Finally, Aletha downloaded. "How dare you, motherfucker? How fucking dare you defy us? After all we'd done for you? We *created* you. You have defied your Creators. Do you get that? We may not stop whipping you until you're dead."

I reached for subspace, reached and reached – but the pain was too great. I started to cry.

My tears excited them to greater frenzy. When I screamed, Roger slapped a ball gag into my mouth.

At some point, I passed out from the pain. At the portal of death, there were no thoughts. I had moved beyond concepts.

When my eyes opened, they were still there looking at me with disgust. There was blood all over the bedspread. I couldn't move a toe without excruciating pain.

"What the fuck happened, Pamela?" Aletha asked.

"I switched on him, Aletha. I snapped one of your electric cock cages on his cock and ball. A little taste of its potential, and he agreed to recuse himself. He'll let the progressive lower court rulings stand."

"Really? You did that Pamela? I'm impressed." Was she being sarcastic? I couldn't tell. "You accomplished your short-term goal. If he honors his agreement."

"If he doesn't, he'll receive the shock of his life – in public, on the bench."

"How do you know he hasn't had the cage removed?"

I looked at her. "Did I have my cage removed?"

"He's not you."

"He won't."

"And what about me, Pamela? What about my mission? All the energy I put into having you fulfill it? I wanted him dead. Plus, next month he'll just revert to his reactionary ways."

"I'm sorry, Aletha. I discovered I'm not a killer. Maybe you should just kill him yourself."

"I would – but I can't get near him."

I looked over at Roger.

Aletha glanced at him as well. "Roger's no killer either. He even talked me out of killing you."

"I'm done, Aletha. Go ahead if you want to kill me. This whole project was supposed to end with my meaningful death. Yet I'm still here."

"Maybe death is too good for you." Aletha's voice seemed to rattle up from the bowels of the earth. "Let's see if the Justice lives up to his agreement. What will you do if he ends up voting the wrong way?"

"I'll turn the unit all the way up until he collapses on the bench. They'll rush him to the hospital and find the cock cage. How will he explain that?"

"Don't be naïve, Pamela. They have ways of covering up all kinds of scandals. He'll just call Olivia Pope."

"I could blackmail him. We do have the video."

Aletha and Roger looked at each other and smiled. "We would love to watch your performance, Pamela. Give it to me."

I looked at her, eyebrows raised. I was still hog-tied, though the position felt so natural I had practically forgotten. I was an immovable sphere rolling around on the bed like a giant beach ball.

Roger untied me. Our eyes met. He'd been quiet. Something zapped between us.

"We can watch it now," I was eager for the distraction. I creaked my ravaged body over to my fanny pack and inserted the camera into the hotel's 50-inch flat screen. I fast forwarded past the dead space while I waited for Sylvester to make his entrance. I dozed off.

When I woke up, we could see him but not me. I was on the head shitting my guts out. But I returned with my mountain lion pounce and magnificent clobber of Sylvester's head.

They applauded my performance. "Go, Pamela," Roger shouted. We watched as I tied Sylvester spread-eagled to the bed. As I attached the cock cage. As I dropped my scrotum such as it was in his mouth.

Aletha said, "Wow, Pamela, you've become quite the Domme!"

In that moment, I fully woke up. More awake than I'd ever been. Destroyed as my body was. I commanded, "Turn it off," the voice from deep in my viscera. Aletha hit the remote.

They looked at me. I stared back. Their eyes were full of fear. The yearning to surrender.

I stared, a glaring eye on each of them. I focused on Aletha, the one who started it all. "Take off your clothes, Aletha." She hesitated and then acquiesced like a timid third grader.

My submission had reached its nadir and my consciousness rebounded. Like a Fourth of July skyrocket, astrocytes bursting in the air, power emanating from my body. I was about to change history. I could do anything.

"Assume the position," I commanded.

She scrambled to kneeling her ass in the air, face in the pillow. My cock assumed its position. I giggled as I knelt behind her. I spanked Aletha with Roger's measured rhythm, alternating between her cheeks.

I retrieved a riding crop with a little pink leather heart at the business end from Roger's bag and whipped her cheeks, one then the other. "Raw hamburger meat," I whispered.

I lubed her asshole. I fucked her until she came. I spurted my spunk inside her.

The afterglow was a new level of heaven. I had never felt so powerful. I had never felt so responsible. The fullness of both yin and yang at the same time. The circle's complementarity fulfilled. Life's complementarity fulfilled.

Aletha smiled, bowed with a *namaste* gesture. She dressed quickly, grabbed Roger's hand, and left without another word.

19

Day in Court

The last day of the Supreme Court term was hot, humid, grey, oppressive as only the marshy South can be in summer. I arrived at the Supreme Court Building at 7:00 in a pink oxford-cloth button down shirt (from Costco, not Brooks Brothers) and no-iron khakis. My non-descript look.

To be sure he didn't lose sight of our agreement, I sent Sylvester a jolt.

There was already a line around the block. I recognized some movement people, but I covered my face with my hand and went straight to the head of the line. I showed the red paper ticket to the Security Guard. He lined up the 50 who would be seated in the gallery, with me in front. After a short wait, they directed us through the metal detector.

We had to wait at the door of the courtroom itself for another hour with another bunch of VIPs. I recognized some Senators and such. My stomach felt infested with hummingbirds. Concerned about being ejected like I was on my first visit the court, I attempted to remain invisible.

I had a pang of guilt as I reflected about the past 72

hours – it seemed politically incorrect to have dominated three Black people. I've always abhorred situations where the male dominant and the female submissive reinforced oppressive sexist relations. But it was clear that domming someone is the ultimate submission. By sharing these fantasies and acting them out, I had reached an intimacy that would have been hard to imagine before. Deep down, everyone craves the sensation of complete surrender. Trusting absolutely, even as your Dom hurts you. Was this type of fantasy play therapeutic? Or was it that – as Aletha said over and over – you like what you like?

I checked Facebook. There were pictures of demonstrators surrounding the White House, the Capitol, and the Supreme Court. Unreliable estimates said over 100,000 people.

The Court police took us to a bank of lockers and instructed us to lock away cell phones – everything but a pen and pad of paper. How had I not remembered this? Before closing the locker, I gave Sylvester a long blast of juice.

They ran us through one more metal detector and then opened the doors to the courtroom. There was a rush for seats, but the front row filled last, so I chose the right side as close to Sylvester's chair as protocol permitted, separated by the gaggle of lawyers.

The rest of the room was filled with dignitaries and officials. I didn't see another movement person. The buzz was what you'd expect of an audience waiting for the movie to begin. Was there a sense of history in the making? Perhaps not, since the outcome of these cases was considered inevitable.

At 10 o'clock, the Marshal pounded his gavel and shouted "All rise." The audience watched a line in black robes file in from the back and take their places on the bench as the marshal voiced the traditional chant: "The Honorable Chief Justice and the Associate Justices of the Supreme Court of the United States. Oyez! Oyez! Oyez! All persons having business before the Honorable, the Supreme Court of the United States, are admonished to draw near and give their attention, for the Court is now sitting. God save the United States and this Honorable Court!"

But there were only eight Justices present. Sylvester Johnson was conspicuous in his absence. A murmur rippled through the audience.

The Chief Justice stood and looked over the room "We have an unusual situation. Justice Johnson has suffered a sailing accident which has resulted in a severe concussion. He is currently in the hospital. He has been forced to recuse himself from all four of the decisions."

The courtroom stirred with astonishment.

"Therefore, in the case of *Williams v. Florida*, the judgment is affirmed by an equally divided court.

"In the case of *Doe v. Virginia*, the judgment is affirmed by an equally divided court.

"In the case of *Richmond v. Chevron*, the judgment is affirmed by an equally divided court.

"In the case of *The Coalition of Cancer Cooperatives v. the United States of America*, the judgment is affirmed by an equally divided court.

"There being no further statements from the Justices at this time, this court is adjourned." The Justices stood and marched behind the burgundy curtain.

The decorum of the court broke down and pandemonium broke out. Who could believe what had just happened, except me. Yes! What occupied my mind was how the hospital dealt with his cock cage.

The massive demonstration outside was jubilant. I could walk through it with impunity, knowing the people who would suspect me of betraying the cause were in jail.

20

Redbone II

I slept twice around the clock at the Capitol Hotel. I wanted to call Matthew, but I was scared shitless. The next day I ran into him at our Starbucks. We were both NOT-looking for each other.

I was in line as he came in the door. He walked right up to me, his fists balled, his chin stuck out. "Peter!"

"Hi, Matthew," I looked at the floor, submissive again.

"You're a snitch, Peter."

"It's not what you think. I'm the one who got Johnson to recuse himself. I'm the reason we won."

"Really, Peter?" He cocked his head skeptically.

How much could I tell? What was my story? "I'm the one who hit him on the head."

He tried looking deeper into me. "I'm sorry I misjudged you, Peter. You're a raving lunatic."

"You have to believe me."

"I don't share that obligation. How would you have gotten that close to Johnson?"

If he only knew how close. "I stowed away on his boat."

Another look. "Nah. I don't know what happened to Johnson, but I know for certain that it wasn't that. I get that you're crazy, probably from the guilt of ratting us out. Celia thinks we should kill you."

"I suppose I couldn't blame you, thinking what you think. It's true I told them where the meeting was, but it was after I was sure we would win all four decisions."

"And you knew this how?"

"He – Sylvester Johnson himself – promised."

The skeptical look chilled to a cold stare. "There's stuff you're not telling me, but the most logical conclusion is that you are totally bonkers, that something happened to you. Meanwhile, I would advise you to disappear. Like now. Other people with less compassion than me are looking for you. And I never want to see you again."

I shuddered. Tears welled up on me. If only I could tell him the whole story, but he still wouldn't believe me. I don't think I'd believe me.

I took his advice. I left Starbucks without even scoring my venti mocha.

California here I come. I returned to the hotel, packed up my stuff and caught the Metro for the airport. I bought a first-class American Airlines nonstop ticket to Oakland for $1979, leaving in two hours.

I called Mariana. "Hi."

"Hello, Peter." Cold, businesslike.

"I told you this would happen."

"You told me what would happen?"

"That I would get Sylvester Johnson to recuse himself on the four decisions.

Silence. Softening her tone: "Peter, are you seeing a counselor or something?"

"No. Why?"

"Oh, no reason, except that you're totally delusional. Quite possibly a danger to yourself and others."

My turn for silence. "Okay. Well, I'm coming to Oakland. You can see me or not. Once you hear the whole story, you'll believe me." I wasn't at all sure this was true, or even that I could tell her anywhere near the whole story.

"I guess I can't stop you from coming to Oakland. You can't stay here, though. I hope I don't need to get a restraining order."

Ouch. Deep breath. "Okay. I'll call you once I'm settled." Motel 6, here I come.

In the boarding area, a profound sense of well-being settled into me. I'd done something kind of cool. Something that changed history. Without anyone beyond Aretha and Roger – and Sylvester – even knowing about it.

Just as the loudspeaker announced the boarding of first class passengers (that's me!) Thing One and Thing Two approached. My new BFFs.

"I'm afraid you need to come with us Peter. We have to turn you over to the federal marshals. You're wanted for suspected terrorism."

"Hey, we had a deal!"

"We did, and we feel terrible about having to renege. Someone way over our heads nixed the deal."

My companions turned me into the federal marshals in their own office at the airport. The marshals were so nondescript – so nice, polite, and respectful – that I can't tell you what they looked like. They read me my rights. I was in a fog. Thinking trivial things – would I get a refund back on my ticket? Resigned to my fate.

They took me to the Central Detention Facility, not one of the precincts like last time. The intake procedure was light-years different. I was treated like a Goldman-Sachs VIP caught for insider trading. When they strip-searched me, they didn't even glance at my violet lace panties, let me keep them on. The orange suit they gave me fit stylishly. No holes in the back.

My cell was painted a cheery yellow, spacious, twin cots. "Will I have a roommate?" I asked the earnest, baby-faced guard.

"Yes, he's on the yard. Be back shortly."

"Welcome home," the guard said in parting.

"And my key?" I joked.

He laughed. "I wish I could."

I lay back on the three-inch mattress. Not Tempur-Pedic. I settled into my new home.

As I was dozed off, the iron door opened, my roommate filling the opening. "Peter," he shouted in his James Earl Jones voice.

"Redbone." We did a man-hug, punching each other's backs while the guard slammed the door with its doom-filled clang. My whole body returned his smile.

We sat facing each other, staring affectionately into each other's eyes.

"You didn't engineer this, did you Redbone?"

"Me? How could I do such a thing? I mean I do follow the news. And I have a lot of friends, some of whom owe me."

I stiffened. "It's not like I was in the papers or anything."

He gave me a cryptic smile.

It took my paranoia a couple of days to warm back up to Redbone. I would never know how we came to be stuck together, but it didn't matter. Nothing mattered anymore. And that felt liberating.

On the second day, the guard took me to the infirmary, to a very small, elderly doctor with a thick Eastern European accent. "Ve understand you haf astrocytoma. You haf been chosen to participate in an experimental trial using stem cells from an embryo created in part from you own sperm." She gave me a cup. "You are very lucky, Peter. You must haf friends in high places for this to happen so fast. This procedure has just been cleared by the Supreme Court. Please ejaculate into this cup."

I went to the bathroom and did as she asked without difficulty. Smiling, I returned the cup to her. "In five days, ve vill inject you with the stem cells."

I'm going to live!

Halfway back to my cell, another cosmic headache came on like a steam roller crushing my brain. I had to sit down. Immediately my consciousness dropped down to the cellular level. I don't know what it looked like to the guard, but I was floating on the battle plane of PDF and TBC. The stem cell army was partying, which they do by rapidly transforming themselves as different kinds of cells, like a role-playing game.

The motionless mound of astrocytoma cells, soccer balls with nails sticking out of them, gave off a sullen vibe, as if their defeat was imminent.

Frank waved at me from up in the sky of this miniature universe – far away, a mere dot among dots. "See you later!" he messaged me, acknowledging that I wouldn't be dying this time around.

On the third day of automotoning through the prison routine, of being simply roommate-cordial to Redbone while he patiently waited, I started to talk. I told him everything, pouring my heart out non-stop for a good hour and a half as we lay on our cots. From the planning stages to the delicious kinkiness. I started getting off, telling the story like the narrator of *100 Days of Sodom*.

Redbone didn't say much through the telling of my story – a few polite *Wows* and *Go on, Bros*. He didn't doubt a word I said. When I got to the part about Matthew not believing me, I was spent.

"That's quite a story, Peter! You're this hero – but you can't tell anyone. Except me of course. Thank you, Peter. I'm honored."

We lay back on our cots and breathed together for a while. Then Redbone whispered, "Peter, come here."

I didn't hesitate. I jumped over to his bed and lay down on top of his husky half-back frame. We kissed. We entwined our tongues. We rubbed all over each other. We wrangled out of our jumpsuits. I in my panties and he naked, we continued writhing. We barely touched each other's cocks before we came together, our cum spurting on our stomachs as we rubbed them together side by side.

I slept in his arms that night. I don't think I ever felt closer to anyone.

CPSIA information can be obtained
at www.ICGtesting.com
Printed in the USA
FSHW02n2331181018
53087FS